The
GEMS
Of
Zephron

Charlize Worthington

ISBN: 978-1-4669-5327-7 (sc)
ISBN: 978-1-4669-5326-0 (e)

Trafford rev. 08/16/2012

 www.trafford.com

North America & international
toll-free: 1 888 232 4444 (USA & Canada)
phone: 250 383 6864 ♦ fax: 812 355 4082

CHAPTER ONE

The Threat To Zephron

*L*yssa Zarift ready herself for the battle to come. Braiding her hair, she placed her golden halo around her head. This would ensure that if they lost the battle and they were captured she would be given immunity. Dressing in the black and dark blue synthetic suit, she began strapping on her weapons. She wore her sword down her back sheathed in leather. Strapping her guns around her thighs, she then added the small daggers to her boots. Around her waist she placed the stun grenades. She was the second daughter of King Zarift and that position made her responsible for the warriors of Zarift.

The warriors of Zarift were few and far between several years ago many of the male population of Zarift had caught a disease that wiped out thirty five percent of the men. Her warrior band was small in numbers she only had hundred warriors in her command. She wasn't looking forward to this attack but yet she had to uphold her father's honor. Even though she wasn't a male it had always fallen to the second royal child, female or male, to be the commander.

King Zarift had received a communications from Zephron stating his fury at having the gems stolen. Zariftian should prepare for war. Zephron was declaring war against the Zarifts the gems were rare to only Zephron's planet. Supposedly someone from Zarift had stolen them and King Zephron wanted them back.

Princess Tess was promised to Prince Voltron their marriage would form a political alliance with Zephron giving Zarift them the right to mine the gems to power their warships.

It angered Lyssa that Zephronians hoarded these gems and would not let other galactic planets use its rare power. Going to war over these gems is not what she wanted and she knew her warriors would probably come out in the end defeated. This didn't set well with her but she had done all she could to train them now it was up to them to meet the challenge. No matter what the outcome of this war she would not let her father down. Looking one last time at herself in the mirror she turned and walked out of the room.

Voltron hated war, he had never agreed to waging this war, it would be a total slaughter of the Zariftian warriors and he was heartsick. The Zarifts had no idea of the destructive power of the gems. Zephronians would not make weapons out of the gems because of the unstable power they caused when used. He could not imagine who would steal the gems or how they would have gotten them without inside information. It had to be some traitor from Zephron.

They should have just waited until his marriage to Princess Tess? Then they would have been given the rights to mine the gems and all its technology except the technology to fashion a weapon out of them. By taking the gems off Zephron the Zephronians would only believe that their intentions was to build a weapon to conquer their universe, the line had been drawn, war was inevitable. Voltron's father was furious, why did King Zarift insist they go to war? Just because Zephronians did not share the rare gem with neighboring planets had nothing to do with the technology for powering up a starship. It was because of its capacity to make dangerous weapons. Teaching the Zarifts how to mine and use the gems for space travel was a part of the marriage alliance. King Zephron could assume that stealing the gem had more to do with using the gems to make powerful dangerous weapons.

Putting on his battle uniform, he began placing his weapons on himself. He placed his golden wreath crown on his head. He placed his grandfather's sword around his waist. He held it almost reverently, he had loved his grandfather. When his grandfather had died in an attack, his sword had fallen to the eldest grandson. He had promised his grandfather that this sword would only be used to protect his family. Now here he was going to war to protect his family against those who would make weapons of destruction. Voltron knew he would fight to protect his people even though he knew in his heart the Zarifts didn't have a chance.

Leaving Varian Zephron's military outpost the warriors transported to the warship the Erne and headed for the orbit of Zephron. Two days later the Zarifts attacked with a vengeance, hitting the Zephronians hard. They managed to take out the outer barrier of their protected City of Zephrite. Voltron was on the warship when the battle report came in. Running to the transporter he barked out commands to his crew as he and his warrior group transported to the surface of Zephron. Arriving on the surface he looked around there were several Zarifts lying dead, but a larger group was using a weapon to try and penetrate the walls of the city. Unsheathing his sword Voltron roared as he rushed into battle to take the group of Zarifts using the weapon.

Lyssa barked orders to her warriors to hold their ground. Hearing a roar she turned to find the tallest Zephronian she had ever seen come roaring into their midst. Unsheathing her sword she rushed at him ready to take him out. It took Voltron by surprise that a woman would be fighting in this conflict. He let his guard down and at that moment she attacked violently slicing Voltron across his midsection, stunned Voltron staggered back, anger in his eyes as he realized she was serious about doing him harm. Before the warrior could recover though she raised her sword a second time and brought it straight down on his shoulder he bellowed in pain and grabbed her by the arm nearly crushing it with his strength. Surprised and shocked that he still had such strength after she had severely wounded him her mind reeled with the thought that maybe all Zarifts would die this day. Shaking her as if she had no substance at all he raised his hand and back handed her knocking her unconscious. Her crown had fallen off in the attack on Voltron he had no idea that she was a Princess of Zarift.

Looking around seeing that the weapon had been disabled and that the attack was winding down and the Zarifts were few in number now, Voltron's adrenaline was ebbing and he began to feel lightheaded. Picking up the woman he pressed his com and was immediately transported to his ship. In the transportation bay Voltron fell to his knees, the blood loss was extensive. The last thing he recalled was telling his men not to harm the woman and to lock her in his quarters.

Healer Belgorod looked at Voltron one more time, he had done his best and the robotic medical unit had stitched and repaired the torn skin and ligaments and then had replaced the blood that he had lost. Turning to MAILS he told the computer to send for Voltron's second in command.

"How is he?" Betel asked the healer. "He's better however he's lost a lot of blood and will need much rest. His shoulder was badly injured. He is lucky that the blade had not severed the tendon. Tell Arielle not to worry."

Running his hands through his hair Betel shook his head glad that his friend had not been injured worse. "I will have Arielle inform King Zephron of Voltron's condition." Nodding his head he turned and left the sick bay. There was nothing left for Belgorod to do but to allow Voltron to sleep. He and the nurse in sick bay used the robotic medical transport to take Voltron to his room.

Her head was throbbing as she awoke looking around she was confused. *Where am I? Did I kill the tall Zephronian warrior? This doesn't look like a holding cell. Where am I? Why did my jaw hurt so much?* Then she remembered the tall warrior had hit her after she had attacked him. Rising she walking around the room it was quite spacious for a holding cell. There was a food replicator here a cleansing chamber and a large very large bed. *I do not know how long I have been here but the next person through that door was going to hear an earful from me.*

Just about that time Healer Belgorod and the nurse brought Voltron into his quarters. He knew that there was a woman on board. This must be the one that had attacked Voltron. "Well hello my dear. I am Healer Belgorod." He addressed her and smiled at her guiding the medical cart toward the bed with the help of the nurse.

"Don't hello me. How dare you keep me locked in this room, I am Princess Lyssa of Zarift and by the galactic code I should be returned to my planet by now!" she shouted at the healer.

"Are you really a Princess of Zarift? If you are a princess where is your crown?" He asked her noting her anger.

"It's right here on my head you, you barbarian." Reaching up to show him her royal head band she realized it was no longer on her head. She paled at this realization, how was she supposed to convince them she was a princess without her royal head band. "It must have gotten lost in the skirmish." She said.

"Yes I thought as much, I heard that the woman being held in Voltron's room was the one that had attacked him. Princess' don't fight in battles."

"You stupid Zephronian, on my planet women fight alongside their men, since I am the commander of Zarift warriors I am obliged to fight alongside them." She snapped back

Laying Voltron on the bed he pressed the robots button to withdraw the floating medical cart. Dismissing the nurse he covered Voltron with one of the blankets off the bed leaving the sheet on him as well. Calming down enough to actually see what the healer was doing she was stunned to see the warrior she had attacked still unconscious. Going to the side of the bed she looked down at this tall Zephronian, he was not bad to look at and in a way she was glad he was not dead, now she could really take her vengeance out on him. Standing by the bed she continued to look down at this man, he was tall with dark blue/black hair that came down to his shoulders. His face was pale but that could be due to blood loss. His face was handsomely rugged. Pulling her eyes away she heard the healer speaking, he acted like he knew what she was thinking. Eyeing her wearily he spoke to her he said, "He needs to rest. He lost a lot of blood and the injury to his left arm is quite extensive." He turned to leave, stopping at the door he spoke to MAILS, "Keep an eye on her, and notify me immediately when he wakes." Then he left.

Going to the bridge, Belgorod told Betel that Voltron had been taken back to his quarters. "I am having MAILS monitor Voltron just in case that woman attacks him again." Turning to Arielle he spoke, "Arielle you can check on him later, let him get some rest now.

Rising from the command chair Betel said, "You have the bridge Maddox. Orin plot coordinates for Varian." Turning to Arielle, "Send a communication to King Zephron telling him we are heading back to Varian." Walking to the transporter he spoke, "Deck 4."

Betel arrived at Voltron's quarters a few minutes later. Standing, in the farthest corner of the bedroom, was Lyssa. He spoke to her, "I am glad to see you are standing in the farthest corner away from him. What were you doing fight in the skirmish?" He asked.

I am Princess Lyssa of Zarift commander of the Zariftian Warriors." She snarled.

"Really where is your crown if you are a princess?" He challenged.

"I lost it in the skirmish on Zephron." She glared at him.

Snorting he said "I don't believe you. You are saying that to get away from being held captive." He snarled.

Sparks flying from her eyes she spoke, "How dare you call me a liar, pod-cast my father and ask him who I am. I will not attack him if he doesn't attack me." She stated.

Looking at her covered with blood and dirt he pointed to the cleansing chamber. "You may use the cleansing chamber you are covered by blood. When you are done showering, food will be brought to you. If you attack him again," he indicated Voltron, "you will be taken to the cargo bay and my men will use you as they will."

Her face paled, but she stood her ground. She was not about to let this oaf think he had frightened her. His eyes narrowed, snarling he spoke softly, "You will bathe and you will not attack him!" As he finished he showed her the cleaning chamber, threatening to undress her himself if she didn't bath. Jerking away from him she glared at him daring him to do so. Stepping forward Betel did not back down ready to follow through with his threat. Inhaling sharply she quickly dove through the cleansing chamber doors as they opened.

Lyssa stripped off her dirty blood stained clothes and tossed them into the cleaning tube. Walking into the stall she unbraided her hair, she relaxed as warm water and cleaning solution rinsed her up and down. Holding her head back she turned to let her long blonde hair get more of the cleaning solution in order to clean it. Hitting the button one more time, warm water pulsed down her long hair getting out the blood and dirt. Hitting the drying button Lyssa slowly turned to allow the pressurized air to dry her completely. She felt refreshed and stepped out of the stall. It dawned on her that she had nothing to wear as she kicked the cleaning tube where her dirty clothes were. In her anger she hurt her big toe bending to grab it she lost her balance. She then bumped her bottom into the opposite wall activating the drawer panel button. It popped opened and pushed her forward quickly. Stumbling she fell to the floor with a yelp as she hit her head on the shower stall frame. Rolling over and trying to get up off the floor, the cleansing chamber doors suddenly swished open.

Voltron stood in the doorway, "What in the blazes is going on in here?" He rubbed his blurry eyes trying to focus on the naked woman on the floor. Frowning he tried to remember when he had brought her aboard. Gasping she realized he was naked. When he realized she was trying to get up he bent over to help and all the blood left his head. Feeling dizzy he looked at her one more time before he went unconscious, landing on Lyssa's five foot four inch frame pinning her underneath him. He landed squarely between her legs. Squirming she tried to push him off her, but he was much too heavy and she realized he wasn't going anywhere. *Oh great, now what am I going to do. I can't believe this. Didn't Belgorod tell the medical artificial intelligent life system to wake him when the warrior awoke? Well maybe he would be here soon and he could get him off me.* Then the thought hit her *oh my, I am naked I can't have the healer seeing me like this.* So with renewed vigor she tried once more to push him off of her it didn't work, it only made matters worse as he slid down her body trapping his shaft against her sex causing her to gasp. She had decided that moving any more would be disastrous. *Drumming her fingers on his back she thought what am I going to do now lying back she decided she might as well try and rest.*

Voltron breathed deeply smelling his mates scent. Groaning he caressed her skin as he spoke tender words of love to her. Running his hands through her hair he called out to her.

"Elena my love." He wanted to kiss her and nuzzle her neck. He could smell her arousal and it ignited at his passion. Finding her lips once again he kissed her softly at first waiting for her lips to open so he could explore her mouth with his tongue. Heat started building up in his lower belly, he felt as if he hadn't mated with Elena in several moon cycles.

Finding her breasts he cupped each one tenderly, rubbing his thumb over her swollen nipple. Leaving her mouth he found her puckered nipple and began sucking in earnest. Hearing her soft moan drove him on. He lowered his hands to the place between her legs. Rubbing his finger over her tender flesh a moan escaped him. She was already wet for him. He needed her so badly. Her legs were already spread for him waiting for him to enter her. Pushing his turgid shaft against her opening he couldn't resist any longer. With a quick shove he was in her. She stiffened and cried out, why? Kissing her softly again he murmured against her lips. "Elena, my love, I have missed you let me love you, let me fill you with my shaft until we both have pleasure.

At first Lyssa enjoyed the lips kissing her, the hands that gently roamed over her. The heat from those hands promised great passion. It was only when Voltron had entered her that she screamed out in pain. Stop, stop her mind screamed, you can't do this, and I am a Princess of Zarift. Pushing she tried to stop him. Her bucking hips only encouraged him to continue their pumping.

He could not understand why Elena was fighting him. He wanted her, his desire for her was too great to stop. Grabbing her arms he held them above her head as he pumped into her. Finding her lips again he kissed her deep. Trailing his kisses down her cheek to her ear where he spoke tenderly to her. "I need you so much." Lyssa's bucking and struggling beneath him only served to inflame his passion. Nearing his release he bit down on her soft shoulder the bite had drawing blood, he quickly sucked on the place kissing it and licking it to seal in the serum he sent into her system. "By all the stars in Zephronian space you are mine. Mine Elena! Shooting his seed deep inside her Voltron collapsed again. This time he rolled off her releasing her from his weight.

Biting her lip Lyssa rolled away from him as he released her. She sat there looking at the unconscious warrior lying on the floor. Jumping up she felt something sticky between her legs looking down she saw blood, evidence of her lost purity. Gasping, Lyssa put her hand to her mouth, *what now, what am I to do,* running from the cleansing chamber she sought the far side of his bed where she collapsed on the floor crying out in her anguish.

Sobbing, she cried for the loss of her innocence. She cried so hard and so long that she finally fell asleep rolled into a ball on the floor.

"What the hell?" exclaimed Belgorod, as he walked into Voltron's quarters that morning and found the bed empty. Movement in the cleansing chamber caught his eye, he found Voltron lying on the floor. "MAILS, why didn't you call me when Voltron awoke?" Hitting the communication device the healer summoned the medical team. "Sorry healer I didn't hear him rise." Shaking his head Belgorod hit the com link. "Commander Betel, Voltron has reopened his wounds and the young woman is no longer in his quarters."

Running from the bridge, Betel sailed passed crewmen as he ran into the elevator, giving the command, "Deck 4." By the time Betel arrived at Voltron's quarters the healer and two sick bay nurses were there placing the floating medical cart at Voltron's head lifting him up off the floor. "Where is that Zariftian bitch, she did this?" yelled Betel. Turning to the two crewmen that had followed him he snarled, "Find her!" Pulling out their stun guns the two left to search the other decks for the woman.

Sliding underneath the bed, Lyssa lay very still she had awoke to screaming men. Then she heard one calling her names. They thought she had escaped. Well she hadn't yet, but as soon as they left this room she would be gone, stopping only long enough in the cleansing chamber to grab some clothes. She didn't have time to think of how she was going to get off this ship, all she knew was that she was going to get off the ship if it was the last thing she did and it might be just that.

She waited until they had placed the warrior on the floating medical bed, as the healer and the sick bay crew left the room she waited only long enough to hear the door swish close. Scrambling out from under the bed she ran to the cleansing chamber and hit the panel where the drawer had popped out yesterday when she had hit it with her bottom. Pulling out a long shirt she quickly donned it and realized it was three sizes too large.

Searching frantically she found a belt and to her surprise she found a dagger as well. She tied the belt around her waist. Quickly going back to the room she grabbed her boots. Putting them on she dashed from the room only to run head first into Betel's arms.

"No, no," she screamed, "let me go." She kicked out and flailed her arms as the tall warrior picked her up and took her back into Voltron's room. Betel's temper was already ignited at having found Voltron on the floor. Grabbing her arms and pinning them to her side he spoke very slowly to her. "What did you do to our Prince and commander?" She was still struggling when the words finally penetrated her thoughts. Her head snapped up, "Your Prince?" she asked. Shaking her he said, "Yes you tried to kill him twice. I will see that you are imprisoned and put to death for your assault on him."

"What. That, that's Prince Voltron of Zephron?" she asked shocked. He answered her with a sneer, "Yes. Prince Voltron. Don't act coy with me. You knew who he was when you attacked him on Zephron yesterday."

"I did not know that he was the Prince, and besides," she sneered "he kidnapped me and I am Princess of Zarift." She said crossing her arms over her chest. Glaring at him she decided that not talking right now would be the best thing she could do. They couldn't find out about him raping her. After all it was her sister that Prince Voltron was supposed to marry. Paling suddenly she realized with one clear thought that her sister's intended had mated with her. She was sick to her stomach, why did this have to happen? Feeling a real fear she started to get light headed, she began shaking. She just couldn't think about what had happened between her and Voltron. Lyssa blacked out in Betel's arms.

Losing some of his anger, Betel gently lifted her and placed her on the bed. *What was wrong with her? Did she really think Zephronians to be that barbaric that they would actually imprison or kill a woman?* Hitting the com link he asked Belgorod to come to Voltron's quarters immediately.

The healer used the medical scan unit to check her he was just covering her with a blanket when Betel came in. "She is fine. She has not eaten in a while and she probably needs nourishment. She is also on her womanly cycle. I found blood between her legs and that along with not eating made her pass out. I have ordered her some food from the galley it is being brought as we speak."

"Thanks, my old friend. I didn't mean to scare her with my words regarding Voltron." He said red faced, "I thought she knew I was just angry and that I would not let our men hurt her nor would we imprison her. Please make sure she eats."

Smiling, Belgorod, slapped Betel on the back, "She'll be fine. You can apologize to her tomorrow. Voltron is also fine. His wound did reopen, but nothing that the medical unit couldn't fix. In fact he is sitting up in sick bay waiting to hear a report from you."

Leaving Belgorod to tend to the woman, Betel left to speak to Voltron. Entering sick bay Betel bowed his head to his Prince and then went over to inspect him. "You are well?" he asked.

"Yes. Could you fill me in on what happened after I was transported to the ship?" he asked.

"Apparently, a feisty young woman attacked you and got the better of you." Betel said trying to hide the smile that threatened to break out on his face.

"A woman," he was confused, "A woman, are you . . . I don't, I mean," he stopped midsentence and trying to figure out what had happened. He smiled, remembering a beautiful woman attacking him with her sword. "Yes there was this little spite fire that came running at me with a sword. She took a swing at me and hit me mid chest. I was so stunned that I let my guard down; I didn't see the next move coming. She came straight down on my shoulder with her sword." Grimacing he rubbed his shoulder. "I grabbed her and nearly broker her arm." Groaning he remembered back handing her. Concerned he asked Betel, "Where is she? Is she alright?"

Betel cleared his throat he knew Voltron would not like what he was going to say next, "It appears I have made her pass out." He said as he placed his hands behind him and lowered his head.

"How, what did you do Betel?" Voltron asked worried about the young woman he had brought aboard his ship. She was under his protection and he certainly didn't want his second in command harming her. "Didn't I tell you not to harm her?"

"Yes, and I didn't. When we found you on the floor in your cleansing chamber we thought she had attacked you again. I was worried about you and spoke harshly to her."

He stopped.

"And?" bellowed Voltron.

"And, I told her that If she had reinjured your shoulder that I was going to imprison her and put her to death." Clearing his throat, "of course that was after I had told her not to harm you again. I also told her she would be taken to the cargo bay and my men would use her any way they wanted to if more harm came to you." Betel finished red faced.

"BY ALL THE GALACTIC GODS, Betel, how could you?" Voltron stormed. Betel shrunk away from Voltron's anger. Hanging his head, Betel spoke softly, "I have no excuse Voltron; there was no honor in what I did for that I am truly sorry."

Voltron shook his head, his anger ebbing "Where is she now?"

"She's in your quarters on your bed resting. I will go and make sure she is alright." He turned to leave. Turning back, he spoke. "How soon will you be able to go back to your quarters?" he asked.

"Belgorod said one more unit of blood and I will be strong enough to return to my quarters to rest." The healing unit had finished sealing the wound on his shoulder, "so I will be able to leave soon."

"I will make sure the woman is well taken care of until your return then." With that he left sick bay.

The dish barely missed Betel's head as he started to enter Voltron's room. "I told you, you four eyed, jackass. I do not want to eat."

"Be reasonable," said Calil "the healer has said you must eat." Picking up yet another dish, she threw it at the young crew member who ducked just in time, as the plate hit Betel in the chest.

"Calil, leave us." The young crew member couldn't run out of the room fast enough. "Do not touch me," Screamed Lyssa at Betel as she picked up another dish to throw at him.

With hands held up palms forward the universal sign for peace he spoke, "I will not harm you. I have come to offer my apologies to you."

Lyssa glared at him, "What?"

"I have come to offer you my apologies, I have gone against my Prince's orders not to harm you. I did not mean to make you think that we would punish you for harming Voltron. We would never hurt a woman," swallowing Betel bowed his head waiting for her to reply.

"What did you say?" she asked.

"Voltron had ordered that we not harm you for hurting him. When the transporter brought both of you up from the surface of the planet he told us to take care of you just before he passed out."

"He did?"

"Yes he did, and I disobeyed his orders and caused you to believe that we would harm you, and for that I am truly sorry and ashamed. There was no honor in what I did."

Voltron entered the room quietly. He saw the young woman in his bed and his interest was piqued. He watched her as she spoke with Betel. Her long beautiful blonde hair flowed down her back. She had his tunic on and that made him smile that she would even dare to wear his clothes.

Betel saw Voltron and smiled, "I have apologized to her my Prince but she has not forgiven me."

Lyssa face reddened at that statement, and she cleared her throat, "I forgive you mighty warrior." Bowing her head to him, she had acknowledged that she truly did forgive him. Betel bowed his head to her acknowledging her forgiveness, he then turned and bowed his head to Voltron and left.

Walking to the bed Voltron lay down beside her. Turning on his side toward her he asked, "What is your name little one?"

Mesmerized by his soft lips and beautiful blue eyes rimmed with silver she could almost lose herself in those eyes, she almost forgot to answer him. "Well," he said "are you going to tell me or not?"

"Oh, yes, I am Lyssa," she spoke softly.

Pulling her into his arms he drew her body next to his. Gasping she tried to resist but even injured he was still too strong for her. "Please do not struggle I am too tired to fight you. I just want you near me as I sleep." Laying his head next to hers, he closed his eyes and was instantly asleep.

Not again. I can't believe I am lying by him again. It could be worse though, he could be naked. Giggling she was glad he was fully clothed. He roused at the sound, rolling toward her even more, almost on top of her. Inhaling sharply she tried to scoot away but he just tightened his hold on her. Finally giving up she relaxed against him. She wasn't really tired but this was better than pacing the floor waiting for him to wake. She spoke softly, "Computer. Play music."

"Is there any songs in particular"

"Anything is fine," She yawned. "Something soft I think."

Beautiful music filled the chamber. She didn't know this song but she instantly liked it. "Yes, that is fine," she smiled as the wonderful music played.

In no time at all she was sleeping as peacefully as Voltron.

Again he held Elena in his arms. Nuzzling her neck he spoke soft words of love to her. "Why did you leave me Elena? I died a thousand deaths and wished upon every star in the Zephron sky that you hadn't left me." Sighing he nuzzled her hair. This time when he inhaled Elena's scent it was different. Rising above her he tried to focus on her face. The image was blurry. The hands that rose to capture his face felt soft like Elena's and he laid his head back down kissing her cheek. He let his hand roam freely over her soft beautiful curves, stopping to capture her full rounded breast in his hand. Moaning softly he spoke her name, "Elena, Elena." As he held her he could feel her fading away, "No, Elena, stay, do not go." He cried out in anguish. Collapsing on the bed he felt as if his life had left him. Rising quickly he opened his eyes, realizing it had been a dream.

Lyssa lay next to him, tears brimming in her eyes. *He must have loved Elena with all of his heart and soul. Why am I crying it make no sense, I hardly even know this warrior this Voltron.* Looking into his eyes she allowed herself to have feelings for him. *His sensuous lips, soft caresses and loving embraces have my body betraying me. I want to have his hands on my body his lips on mine just thinking like this is causing me to tremble.*

He started to rise from the bed and then remembered he had a young female in his bed, where had she gone. Turning he saw her lying there so small so vulnerable with tears in her eyes. "Did I hurt you?" he questioned

She shook her head no.

"You are crying, why?" he asked concerned that he may have hurt her. Lying back down he pulled her gently to him. Gently wiping away the tears that flowed down her cheeks he spoke to her, "If I did not hurt you then why are you crying?" Just looking at her so small and vulnerable made him want to protect her and keep her from harm.

Trying not to cry she looked at him, "Who is Elena?" she asked softly.

His anger flared, "who told you that name?"

"You spoke her name just now and then last night in the cleansing chamber." Once the words were out of her mouth she could have bit her lip.

Rising up quickly his eye's narrowed as recognition dawned on him. "It was you last night wasn't it? It wasn't a dream. I mounted you and not my mate Elena." Shaking his head he was angry that he didn't have better control of himself.

Of course he had been injured but still he should have better control. Of course he could have better control if his mate had not left him for another. When she had left he promised himself he would never take another mate. Of course mounting her did not mean he would have to mate with her unless . . . he remembered biting her. Hitting the bed beside him he swore out loud.

Lyssa sat up, "yes it was me you raped in the cleansing chamber last night." She yelled angry at him. "What now you get mad?" she asked incredulously.

Standing looking over her he spoke, "I did not rape you intentionally; I thought you were my mate. The mate I loved dearly until she left me to go with another warrior." He spat out. "So do not flatter yourself into thinking I would choose such a small insignificant female, as you to mate with." His words were harsh and cruel. He even grimaced at the harshness of his words.

"How dare you, you barbarian pig." Jumping from the bed she lunged toward him rasing her feet hitting square in the chest attempting to knock him off his feet.

Voltron fell back hitting his head on the wall. Flipping over he snarled at her, and leapt at her with a loud roar. "Trying to kill me again?" He asked raising his eyebrows.

She jumped out of his way as he tried to grab her he ended up with nothing but the sheets that were on the bed. Jumping on his back she pressed her elbow down on his wounded shoulder. Rising from the bed bellowing out in pain, Voltron tried to get her of his back by backing up to the wall and pushing her against it. Sensing what he was going to do Lyssa let go of him and slide to the floor allowing his momentum to carry him in to the wall. Rolling over quickly she swung out with her legs knocking his legs out from under him. His head came down so violently hitting the wall knocking him out.

Rising above him she looked down at him hands on hips, "Damn, what was it with this man and being unconscious." Grabbing his feet she pulled him down from the wall to lay him flat on the floor. Slapping his face she tried to wake him. "How in the hell am I going to get out of this one. Maybe no one would come in and check on him." *Yeah like that will happen.* Swallowing her pride she called out to MAILS, "Prince Voltron has hit his head again. Can you send the healer to his quarters?"

"Oh my Princess Lyssa, what have you done to him?"

"I didn't do, hey, how do you know who I am?" she asked shocked

"I checked your image with the images I pulled into my data base from Zarift." The computer said, "I also know that the commander violated you in the cleansing chamber last night."

"Oh" she groaned "You heard that? You can't say anything about it do you understand? Please tell no one do you understand, MAILS! How did you get into the Zariftian data base?"

"Yes Princess, I will tell no one. Now I will get Healer Belgorod to come to Voltron's quarters. About that database I have to keep some secrets for myself."

Healer Belgorod stood over Voltron shaking his head. "How did he hit his head?"

Gulping she tried to lie but she just couldn't, "He attacked me and I defended myself." She stood her ground she had done nothing wrong. She stood over Voltron with her hands on her hips.

"Well I can't blame you for that. My Prince has never been one to abuse females." Shaking his head, "I am unsure why he is treating you thusly."

"I'm sure your prince has his reasons." She smiled, "After all I did attack him."

Chuckling Belgorod nodded, "Yes there is that small issue." Taking out the transport floating device he placed it at Voltron's head. Pressing buttons the med floating cart he soon had Voltron up and moving. "I will take him to sick bay." Getting to the door Belgorod turned concern on his face. "Forgive me my dear but are you alright?"

Smiling she nodded, "I'm fine, wish I could say the same for your prince."

Walking through the door he guided the cart that held Voltron. Looking down at Prince Voltron he wondered if he needed to be reminded about abusing females. Maybe a few days in the medical unit having several tests done would do him some good. "Come, my prince it is time for your lesson."

Singing and cleaning the quarters for the third time she sat down to determine if they would let her exercise or train. It had been two days since Belgorod took Voltron to sick bay and she was getting restless. "MAILS please ask Betel to come to Voltron's quarters if he isn't too busy." She asked sweetly.

It was five minutes before Betel arrived. "You asked for me?"

"Yes, it has been two days since Belgorod took Voltron to sick bay and . . ." she cleared her throat "I am getting restless. Do you have a training deck on this ship?"

"Yes why?" Betel stood with his hands behind his back.

"Could I . . . Um I mean would you allow me to exercise and train on that deck?" She asked.

Betel looked at this small woman and was furious with his longtime friend and prince. When Belgorod told him that Voltron had attacked her Betel was embarrassed for his friend. Of all people he should obey their laws regarding females. How could Voltron abuse this beautiful young female? Shaking his head he just wanted to knock his friend out for his cruelty to her. "Yes I will have the Warrior Arthur escort you to our training deck." He turned to leave.

"Betel, I thank you very much."

Turning at the door Betel smiled at her. "You are welcome." Returning to the bridge he spoke to Arthur. "You are to escort Lyssa to the training deck. She has requested that she be allowed to train."

"As you command Betel I will go do that now, it time any way for me to train our new warriors." With that Arthur left to retrieve the young female from Voltron's room. He hoped Betel knew what he is doing by allowing her to train with the men.

Her heart rate was high, she had been sparing for sixty minutes. The young warrior that was trying to best her now was breathing heavy. "Come on young one, don't give up now." She spoke laughing

Arthur had stopped his training to watch the match between the small female and one of his younger warriors. She was besting him. He could not take her down even though he had been trying. She had side stepped all his moves and in doing so she had knocked him down several times.

The young warrior glared at the female. He had been taught not to abuse the females, but by the gods of Zephron he wanted to capture her and punish her for her taunting him and besting him. He was embarrassed in front of the other warriors who watched amused. "Do not think your skills are better than mine." He snarled.

"Oh, I do think they are." She taunted him. "You have yet to capture me and take my weapon. When you do then you will have bested me."

Grabbing the wooden pole to attack her with he came at her running ready to swipe her feet out from under her. Jumping at the last minute Lyssa jumped on the young warriors back hitting him hard in the back of his neck. He fell to the mat. Taking her sword she laid it across his backside hitting him hard. Rolling over, the young warrior growled at her. "You do not play fair." Turning her back on the young warrior she was unaware that he had jumped up from the mat.

"That is your problem young one, I am not playing," she threw over her shoulder. The young warrior rushed at her with anger on his face. He would be damned to the fires of Zephron if he allowed a mere female to best him. Taking his wooden staff he raised it above his head and brought it down hard on Lyssa's head. Slowly turning she looked at him with surprise in her eyes before the darkness took her. She barely remembered the screaming Arthur catching her before she hit the mat.

Waking in sick bay Lyssa looked around. Voltron was sitting next to her concern in his eyes.

Rising he went to the bed, "Are you alright?" He asked. "You have been out for several minutes. What were you doing on the training deck?" He asked softly.

"I was restless and needed to exercise. I was sparring with a young warrior named Biden. I think my mouth made him mad." Looking sheepishly at Voltron she asked, "You did not punish him did you?"

Inhaling sharply he spoke angrily to her, "Yes, he is in the holding cells."

"Why?" she asked, "It was not his fault I taunted him. He only did what he was trained to do. It was my fault for turning my back on my enemy."

"Lyssa we are not your enemy." Voltron countered, "Even if we were Biden shouldn't have attacked you from behind. There is no honor in that."

"Yes that is true but I provoked him. Please do not hold him any longer. I am sure he is very upset by his actions." Her eyes pleading with him to grant her this small request of letting Biden go.

The tick in his cheek told her he was still angry. "Raising her hand she touched his arm. Please Voltron let him go and please allow me to continue my training. I cannot stand being confined to a room where I cannot breathe or move."

Running his hands through his hair he let out a long breath, "So, be it. But he will come to you and asked you to forgive his stupidity. That he must do. I guess if you go with me or Betel or even Arthur then you can continue to train."

"I can go by myself!" she exclaimed sitting up in the bed which caused her to reel with dizziness. Laying her head back down she jerked at Voltron anger.

"No you won't if you do not allow one of us to escort you then you will not train. Is that understood?" he stormed.

Nodding she put her hands to head to try and stop the pounding. Closing her eyes she laid back and let sleep over take her. The last thought before she fell into a deep slumber was *as long as I can train.*

It seemed curious that every day it was Voltron who accompanied her to the training deck. He would spar with her. He was amazed at her agility and her powerful strikes with the wooden staff. No wonder she had caught him off guard. She was as good as he was at hand to hand combat. No one could catch her with her side steps, jumps, twirls. She had out witted almost every one of his warriors. He snickered at the embarrassment she caused his men as she adeptly evaded each of their grasps.

Feeling good and tired after her training session she decided to clean up the quarters again. Voltron seemed to be a slovenly person always dropping his clothes and walking away. Of course with him being a prince and all he was probably accustom to someone picking up after him. She on the other hand did not like the special treatment her position in life afforded, she much preferred to take care of her own clothes and clean her room. It was only lately that she had let a maid help out and then the only reason then was the training took up a lot of her time.

Sitting at the table she was singing one of her favorite ballads.

Black, black, black is the color of my true love's hair,

His lips are something wond'rous fair
The purest eyes and the bravest hands,
I love the grass whereon he stands,
I love my love and well he knows,
I love the ground whereon he goes

And if my love no more I see

My life would quickly fade away

Black, black, black is the color of my true love's hair.

She continued to hum the beautiful song and Voltron waited in the alcove listening. Her words went straight to his heart. He shook his head and clenching his fists, no I will not let her in I cannot let her in. Making a noise as if he were just getting to his quarters he called out to her. Quickly Lyssa stopped singing. "Yes I am in here cleaning."

"What you don't have to clean, I have servants to do that sort of thing." He fumed.

Throwing his shirt on the floor she turned angry green eyes to him. "Well excuse me your high mighty prince but it seems you are a bit of a *goha* when it comes to keeping your clothes picked up.

"As I do not have the luxury of being around all the time, duty and that sort of thing," he snapped, "I usually have someone take care of picking up after me. Especially since Elena has left me.

"You are so hard headed." She stormed

"Well you don't listen to a thing I say." He returned stomping his foot.

At that Lyssa started laughing at the two of them, "We sound like spoiled children instead of grown adults. I am sorry Voltron I just can't stand being idle."

Uncrossing his arms he looked at her and said, "Yes I guess I am more tired than I realized. I think I am just going to eat and go to bed. Will you join me?" he asked with a wry smile.

I have a question, why did you bite me the other night? Maybe if you tell me that then I will sleep beside you but nothing more."

"In order for Zephronian females to produce a child the males of our planet has to bite them to make them fertile. It usually takes more than one bite though." He said looking at her.

"You know on my planet we are fertile once we hit our mating age which is eighteen. I just turned eighteen. Maybe I should have the Healer Belgorod give me a physical scan. If I am not with your baby then you could let me go home." She looked into his eyes hopefully.

"No," he shouted, "I will not let you go no matter if you are with my child or without. I like how you pleasure me and I haven't had anyone to do that for several moon cycles." Turning he went into the cleansing chamber to shower.

Taking his shirt she had picked up earlier she wadded it into a ball and threw it on the floor then stomped on it. The insufferable oaf who did he think he was to tell her she would be in his bed because he likes it. *Well I don't like it. I'll show him.* Turning to the door she left she would eat dinner in the dining hall without him.

Turning in the shower he let the hot soapy water run over his skin. Why did she irk him so, *It's because she makes my body feel alive again after Elena. I didn't want to feel those feeling again. But damn the little Carmen she makes my blood boil just looking at her prefect body, the way her breasts feel in my hands they are so round and full, her lips that are made to be kissed. The way her legs wrap themselves around me when I enter her, gods and goddesses what wasn't there to like about her body. Yes I said like I don't love her, I will not love her because it would be too hard to do so again.* Just thinking of her soft breast, her smooth skin made him hard. He needed her to be a release for him and nothing else there just couldn't be anything else. Feeling the stirrings deep in his belly he quickly pressed the compressed air button to dry off. Leaving the chamber he decided he needed her right now and he wasn't going to wait till after he ate.

Walking into the bedroom he looked around and couldn't find her. Thinking she was playing a game he went looking for her. Not finding her in eating area or the large sitting area he become concerned. *Where the hell did she go?* Dawning on him he realized she had left his quarters without him or someone as guard over her. Running back to the bedroom he quickly dressed thinking about where she might have gone he decided the training room was probably her first place she would go. When he didn't find her there he began to worry. Where was she? Where could she go, and then it hit him, she had probably gone to the dining hall. By the gods and goddesses he was going to punish her for being so foolish as to be unguarded on a ship full of male warriors.

The dining hall was filled with several of Voltron's warriors. They were eating, laughing and telling off colored jokes. Just like her warriors she thought with a smiling, suddenly missing them. Getting a plate she went to the food bar to fill it with the savory food she had smelled. The warriors hadn't noticed her at first it wasn't until she sat at one of their tables that all the conversations had stopped. Picking up her fork she looked around, "Something wrong? Is my head screwed on backwards?" taking her fork and spearing a piece of the delicious meat she lifted it in a salute. "Good grub." She said smiling and taking a bite.

Rising Biden went to her table with his tray, "May I sit with you my lady?"

Looking up she smiled and indicated the seat across from her. "How are you Biden?"

"I am well my princess. I wanted to say how much I appreciated your graciousness in asking Prince Voltron to be easy on me I am ashamed and humiliated there is no honor in what I did to you. As young warriors we are taught to handle our anger and I was angry that you a mere woman was beating me at my own training." Taking a drink of his grog he spoke again "Then when I found out that you had ask Prince Voltron to be easy on me because you were taunting me made me feel even more foolish. I am sorrier than you can know."

Smiling at this tall young warrior she said, "Biden I know you would not have attacked me without provocation sometimes my mouth gets me in more trouble than it should. Even my own warriors tell me that sometimes I go too far."

Choking on the fowl he was eating he caught his breath and asked, "You have warrior's?"

Looking at him with frustration she said, "Why do you Zephronians think a woman can't fight or be in command of men. On my planet Zarift the second royal child male or female commands the Kings warriors. Since I am second born I became their commander." Shaking her head she said again, "Why Biden is that so unreal for you and the other men?"

"On our planet women are to be loved, cherished and protected. They do not fight in our wars. They make us our homes and have our babies, and we love them dearly. We will kill another male who attempts to take our mates. That's why I am so surprised."

"Oh, I never knew that about Zephronians." She was about to ask other questions when all hell broke out. She heard a roar and looked up just in time to see Voltron rushing toward them with what looked like feral rage in his eyes. She realized that he was heading straight for Biden. Jumping up and over the table she stood in front of Biden in a crouched position to attack.

Biden turned to the side wondering why Princess Lyssa was jumping over the table what he saw startled him into action. Jumping up he tried to push Lyssa behind him. She pushed him aside and stood her ground.

Crouching down she asked, "Voltron what's wrong?" never taking her eyes off his every move. When she realized he wasn't listening to her she jumped up slamming both feet into his abdomen. He was caught off guard and landed on his bottom. Jumping on top of him she took his face in her hands trying to get through the glaze of rage. "Voltron" she said again, but this time she took his lips and kissed them tenderly." He raised his arms putting them around her. Burying his face in her hair he pleaded, "Don't leave me Lyssa please don't leave me." Looking up she motioned to Biden to take the other warriors and leave. Looking at him she shook her head no. He understood that they were not to mention anything about this to anyone. Quickly and quietly the men left the galley. Ea had seen what was happening and had the presence of mind to close the galley door and secure it as he went back into the cooking chamber. He knew if Lyssa needed him she would call to him.

She remand on the floor holding Voltron rocking back and forth. Raising his head to her she looked at him with more love than she thought she could ever feel for another person. "I'll never leave you Voltron, even though you don't want me I will never leave you like Elena did." Rising off the floor she offered him her hand he feeling ashamed at such display of emotions. Looking at her ruefully he asked, "How many warriors witnessed my humiliation?"

"None they left after I knocked you to the ground." He really didn't believe her but there was very little he could do about it now. "Ea" she said "please open the galley door."

Entering his quarters Lyssa guided him to the cleaning chamber, sitting him on the bench she bent down and took his boots off him, tossing them aside. She unbuttoned his shirt taking it off him. She ran her hands over his face he looked so haggard. She didn't really know how long Elena had been gone but the open wound she left was still not healed. Taking his clothes off him she stripping her shirt off and they entered the shower and activated the water.

"Why did you leave my quarters? Do you know what could have happened to you? Why were you talking to Biden? I don't understand Lyssa are you leaving me like Elena left? He almost sobbed his word.

Kissing him tenderly she placed her hands on his face, "I was angry at you but I would not leave you. I am use to being in the company of warriors they have never hurt me because I have always taken care of myself. Talking with Biden helped me understand that females are treated differently on Zephron. I never meant to cause you this much heart ache. You have repeatedly told me that you do not want me as a mate. Yet tonight you acted like I am your mate." Placing her forehead on his she continued, "You can't continue playing with my heart Voltron. If you can't love me and want me for a mate then put me away from you. If you want me for a mate then things have to change between us."

Putting his arms around her he nuzzled her neck. "I don't mean to be so cruel. Elena put a hole in my heart and it is going to take time to heal." He began rubbing her back up and down liking the feel of her skin.

She hit the water panel again and the warm water ran over both of them she placed her breasts next to his chest and looking into his eyes she kissed him putting all the love and feeling that she could into this one kiss. His heart skipped a beat, "Voltron, I want you, I want to feel your hands on me, I want to make Elena a distant memory for you. You have to let go and let me love you like you should have been loved from the beginning." Her hands massaged his chest and down to his lower abdomen. He stiffened and let out a growl of desire, lifting her he left the shower and went to his bedroom placing her on the sheets. She looked at him so tall, handsome and virile, seeing his hard shaft waiting to love her. She rose on her knees and took his shaft into her hands rubbing him while placing her other hand on his heavy ball sack she gently massaged them. He groaned with desire, pushing her back into the mattress. Lying on top of her he held his weight up with his elbows so she wouldn't be crushed. Pushing her legs apart he sought her sheath with his harden shaft.

She gasped as he entered her. Rising to meet his thrusts she wrapped her legs around his waist. Looking into her eyes he smiled knowing that soon he would bring her the pleasure that she sought as well as the pleasure he wanted. He bent his head down and sucked on her pink ripe nipple. The sucking caused the pleasure to surge to her core, and she rose with a groan of desire. He kept pumping in rhythm and she rose to meet his every thrust, soon the pressure built to a rapturous desire engulfing them both as each found release.

Lying beside her until his breathing returned to normal he looked at her, "I can't promise love just yet but I can promise you that you will be my mate for life Lyssa. I will just have to trust the gods and goddesses that love will come eventually." She looked into his eyes, "If that is all I can have right now it will not be enough."

He rose "I need to be on the bridge I will be back in ninety minutes. Order some food and eat I interrupted your dinner." Turning to go he said over his shoulder, "I . . . well . . . I "he just couldn't get the words out. As a ruling prince and a commander he had never been at a loss for words before he was embarrassed by this and quickly left to dress.

Lyssa laid there her heart tearing apart in her chest. *He can't love me but he wants me as mate only. Can my heart live without love? I don't think so.* Rolling on her side with her back to the cleansing chamber door she didn't bother to roll over when he left. Hearing the swish of both doors Lyssa buried her face into the pillow and cried herself to sleep.

CHAPTER TWO

Choosing a Mate

*N*ow that she had been allowed to train waiting in his quarters was hard to do. Lyssa sat on the bed playing with her long tress winding them around her fingers. *How much longer before one of the men came and took her to training?* Rising she began to pace back and forth. It didn't help much the inactivity drove her crazy. The past few days that she had been allowed to train had not been so bad at least she was able to get out of this room. She was amazed that she hadn't thought of her parents. *How can I think of them when I am in constant turmoil with him?* Shaking her head she went back to sit on the bed. Her thoughts turned to babies and what that would mean to her and to Voltron. *What if I am with child? What would I do? For that matter what would Voltron do?* These thoughts kept her mind busy as she paced back and forth in the small space waiting for them to come and take her to the training deck. *Maybe they will not allow me to train today. They were probably angry with me for causing Voltron another head injury. How was I to know he had a soft head?*

Sighing she turned to the food panel, she was thirsty she asked the computer to get her a drink. MAILS quickly obeyed and the next thing she knew there was a steaming cup of Aleutian tea waiting in the food server for her. Sitting at the small round table in the corner of the room she shipped the tea slowly unaware that Voltron watched her. Clearing his throat he strode into the room.

Startled she turned and looked at him. She rose from the table. She couldn't read what he was feeling. Anger seemed to fill his countenance but not knowing him that well she wasn't sure. Stopping before the food server Voltron ordered a stiff drink. Taking the drink he sat down at the table. "Sit." He barked out the ordered.

Glaring at him she was furious that he thought he could order her around like that.

"Sit!" he growled at her. *What is wrong with me, why am I barking orders to her like she is my servant or one of my warriors?*

Sitting she glared at him with anger in her eyes.

"What am I to do with you Lyssa?" he asked not looking at her.

"Let me go." She stormed.

"Let you go? I am not sure I can do that." He swallowed his drink letting the liquid burn his throat as he did.

"Why when you have said that you did not want another mate. Let me go and I will return to Zarift."

"No." Was all he said rising from the chair he went into the cleansing chamber?

Following him into the chamber she was furious with him and she wanted answers. She stopped short as she saw his nude body in the stall where he was washing. Turning he leered at her. "Care to join me?"

"No, I wouldn't. I want an answer," she demanded. "Why can't you let me go" she fumed at him.

Turning to let the hot water and cleansing solution run down his body he tried to relax.

His whole body ached from the wounds, to his head trauma and now fighting with Lyssa. He just wanted to sleep and relax.

"If you don't love me or want me then let me go?" she stormed stomping her foot.

Hitting the dry button he let the pressurized air dry him. Not caring that he was nude he stepped out of the stall and stood before her in all his naked beauty.

Her breath caught in her throat. He was beautiful from his vivided blue eyes to his dark blue/black shoulder length hair that framed his handsome face. He had silver rims around his blue eyes that she had not noticed before they were so beautiful. In his aroused state the blue in his eyes glowed. He had such wide shoulders and muscular arms, those arms were perfect for holding me, how I wish I could feel those arms around me now. I wish he could love me as he loved Elena. I don't think being just his mate will be enough for me. Her heart broke as she realized that she loved him even if he didn't love her. Letting out a soft sigh she let her eyes continued to travel down his body to his tapered waist, looking lower she saw that he was aroused. His shaft was hard. She caught her breath her heart raced. I want him. I want him to touch me and caress me. I could forgive that he took me without realizing it was me. I remember the exquisite pleasure of those hands they were soft, his kisses so passionate. He is only cruel and hurtful because of what Elena did to him, I would not betray him. Lyssa eyes were glowing with need as she began breathing heavily.

Inhaling deeply he smelled her arousal. Her soft sigh caused his heart to skip. This small female made him tremble almost bringing him to his knees. It was maddening. He did not want to love her yet his body was betraying him as his shaft tightened to the point of being painful. His heart skipped as he felt a deep longing he hadn't felt in several months. The tightening in his groin caused his chest to tighten as well making his breath come out in short rasps. *Why am I affected like this, I am a Zephronian warrior. I have better control than this. Take her,* the small voice in his head said, *smell her need for your body it urged. Pleasure her. Mount her. Do not let her go. Learn to lo . . .* the voice trailed off, his eyes never left hers as he moved to take her into his arms.

Crushing her to him he sought her lips. Kissing her deeply, he groaned softly as she opened her lips to his. Pulling away from his burning lips she begged, "Don't, please stop."

Her struggles only served to excite his already thick shaft making him moan. Pressing into her he wanted to possess her and make her his. He raised his head slightly looking at her. "No, I will not be denied. I smell your need and I will mount you and ease my need." His lips took her softly at first, letting his tongue slide over her softer pink lips teasing and kissing them until they opened again for his tongue to explore her mouth.

Lyssa moaned at his ministrations, she let him kiss her deeply. Putting her hands in his hair she pulled him closer to her. Raising her legs she wrapped them around his waist. Stopping Voltron looked down into the passion filled eyes of Lyssa and groan. He carried her to the bed. Lying her down on the bed he spoke huskily, "Take your clothes off."

Still unsure of her feelings for this man she shook her head no as she clutched her dress to her chest. Reaching for the shirt he took it off her. Gently pushing her back on the bed he lay down on top of her holding his weight up with his elbows and forearms.

Kissing her again he spoke. "I want you so I will take you, you will let me."

She inhaled sharply as the words penetrated her lust filled brain she shouted. "How dare you. Get off me?"

Pressing her deeper into the soft mattress he spoke, "No, Lyssa, I want you, and I smell your arousal, you want me too."

Forcing her legs apart with his knee, the head of his hard shaft nudged up against her sex. Lyssa tried to buck him off her, but only succeeded in making his entrance to her easier. Growling, he slid his ridged shaft into her. Her eyes widened at the sensation. Taking her arms and pinning them above her head with one hand, he used his other hand to find her sex. Gently rubbing her, he knew immediately when she began to give in to the wonderful sensations he was causing.

"No . . . Voltron . . . Please. Please don't" she begged breathing breathlessly again.

"Don't what Lyssa? Do you want me to stop?" He spoke sarcastically, never letting his fingers stop rubbing her nub, causing her to lose her thoughts. "Do you want me to stop or continue?" he asked stopping his wonderful torture.

Pulling out of her he lowered his face to her sex. Inhaling deeply he growled as he fastened his mouth to her sex. Bucking her hips, she was stunned at the power of the desire growing in her core. "You taste so sweet, Lyssa." Licking her nub, he placed his fingers in side her, feeling her muscles tightening. "You are so ready for me little one." Lifting his head he spoke again, this time his voice husky with passion and need. "Do you want me to stop Lyssa?"

So caught up in the rapturous feelings she cried. "No. Please Voltron don't stop." Crying out his name as he stopped the wonderful feelings he was causing in her body.

Smiling knowingly he said, "I thought not." He returned to her to continuing what he had started. Sucking, licking, moving his fingers in and out of her, he felt her body tense. Just as she was about to exploded he stopped. Crying out she tried to grab him and make him continue. Instead he quickly replaced his fingers with his hard shaft. Pushing it deep inside her, he began pumping her, until she cried out his name. Lowering his lips he kissed her tenderly. She tasted herself on his lips.

Slowly he began moving again. His shaft was growing bigger with each thrust inside her, his shaft hot with need. She wrapped her legs around him, clinging to his neck kissing him. Arching her back, he reached down and cupped her breast.

Lowering his head he sucked on one of her puckered nipples. Crying out she moaned against him as her arousal rose again. Pumping faster, Voltron moved his hands to her hips, he held her tightly to him. The head of his shaft buried deep inside her. Roaring out his release, she climaxed with him, holding him closely. He rolled with her onto their sides so he wouldn't crush her with his weight. Slowly their breathing returned to normal.

Caressing her cheek he pulled her tight against him and covered them with the sheet. "I will mount you anytime I want Lyssa. I will mate with you, but I will never love you or anyone ever again." He stated. She stiffened in his arms not believing the words coming from his mouth.

Pushing at his chest he let her go. Rolling to the far side of the massive bed, she turned hate filled eyes on him. "I will never let you pleasure me again. You may take me but I will not respond to your touch. I hate you, you are a barbarian. Let me go to my home planet if you find mating with me to odious." She snarled.

Reaching out for her, his anger over took him and he yanked her back to his side violently, knocking the breath out of her. "I will not let you go

Lyssa. You will be just for me to touch and to find pleasure with. Do you understand?" He growled. When she didn't respond he shook her, "DO YOU UNDERSTAND?" he roared.

Tears began to flow at his words. "Yes, I understand how cruel you will be to me." Pulling herself from his arms she wiped away her tears. "And?" she asked.

"And what?" he countered. Glaring in to her eyes he cocked his head to the side and look at her. It tore at his heart that his words caused her to cry, but he could not let her into his heart. I will not love her no matter how much she pleases me. He could not risk loving her for she would hurt him.

Sitting on her knees she draw herself up she spoke to him "And if I am with your child, what can I expect?" Not looking away she waited for him to respond.

He lay back casually placing his hands behind his head, "If you are with my child it will be taken away after it is birthed. My offspring will be raised in my father's palace on Zephron. You will remain with me." He stated matter-of-factly. She stared at him unbelieving. *How could he be so cruel? I thought when he had found me with Biden and flew into a rage because he thought I was going to leave him had changed him. It hasn't its only made him meaner and crueler.*

"What did Elena do to you to make you so hateful?" she asked softly, tears running down her cheeks.

He started to pull her to him but she jumped from the bed and ran into the cleansing chamber. He didn't bother to follow her. Running his hand through his long blue/black hair he sighed heavily. *I can't love you Lyssa because you will leave me like Elena did. I can't let my heart go through that again. I will not go through that again. I am sorry I didn't mean to be so harsh but I need to make sure you understand me and that I can't ever love anyone again it is just too painful.* Rising from the bed, he pulled on clean pants and shirt, slipping his boots on before he left his quarters. He couldn't stay in there for another minute.

Lyssa heard him leave. Coming out of the cleansing chamber she tore the sheets off the bed and stomped on them. She would show him. "MAILS please ask the healer to come to Voltron's quarters, tell him I have a bad headache."

Entering the room Belgorod noticed the sheets on the floor clearing his throat "What's wrong?" asking softly noticing her red eyes.

"Where I am from when we get ill there is a medication that is given to help with pain and illness. Could you get me some *rugart* medication for my severe headaches? It will help with the pain tremendously." She said rubbing her head making a convincing picture for him of her pain.

Concern etched his eyes. "I do not know of this medication. It is a plant found on your planet?" he asked.

"I did not think you would know of it but I am sure MAILS could synthesize the medication for me." She smiled up at him hoping he bought her lie.

"I will go to sick bay and work with MAILS to make this substance. When it is done I will bring it back to you. I am sure MAILS can make it he is the top of the line in medical artificial intelligence systems." Belgorod left.

"Princess this medication doesn't help headaches. Are you sure you got the right meds?" MAILS asked.

"Yes I have the right medication MAILS."

"But my Princess you know that Voltron will not be happy if you are unresponsive to him."

"I don't give a damn MAILS, he will not hurt me and get away with it. Do you understand, you can't tell the healer what it is I am taking Please." she begged.

"I will not tell Healer Belgorod what the medication really does." MAILS said softly.

She'd teach Voltron a lesson he wouldn't forget in a long time. The medication she was getting would render her libido worthless. Voltron could try till the galactic moons grew dim and he would not be able to arouse her. Smiling she thought *he won't use me for his pleasure. If he can't love me then I will not let my body betray me. I might love him but I won't allow him to hurt me anymore. He will wish he had never met me.* Hesitating she thought about what little she knew of Elena. *Elena had hurt him horribly. I don't want to hurt you I just want to teach you a lesson. It matters to me if you love me or not.* She fumed, *just because Elena hurt him doesn't mean I would have hurt him.*

She knew deep in her heart that she loved him. *I can't help but love him. By all the Zarift moons I will not let my heart love him or be broken by him.* Burying her face in her hands she sobbed her frustrations out. Lying down on the floor she cried herself to sleep.

Belgorod found Lyssa lying on the floor, her eyes red and swollen from her tears. Gently shaking her awake he spoke to her soothingly, "I have your medication for your headache. Do you want to take it now?"

Shaking her head yes Belgorod went to the beverage panel and ordered a glass of cool water. Taking the pills from Belgorod she downed them. Smiling at the kind healer, she returned to the floor to sleep some more. "Why are you on the floor?" Belgorod asked with concern in his voice. She didn't want to explain to the healer Voltron's cruelty. "The bed is too soft. So sometimes lying on the floor helps my back." She lied.

Belgorod started for the door fuming. He saw that her eyes were red and she had been crying. How could Voltron be so heartless? He knew of the laws concerning females and as Prince of Zephron it was his duty to up hold the law. When he came into sick bay the next morning for a recheck of his head, Belgorod would talk to him after all he felt more like an uncle to Voltron than the Healer Belgorod serving on Voltron's warship.

With her knowledge of the medication she knew it would kick in rapidly. One of the side effects of the medication was sleepiness. As she puffed up the pillow and covered herself with the sheets, she smiled, *won't he be surprised when he tries and gets no response sexually from me? This could actually be rather amusing to watch.* It wasn't long before she fell fast asleep.

"Voltron, what are you doing on the bridge?" Betel asked surprised that he would have left his quarters.

"There are too many people in my quarters for me to get adequate rest." He growled.

"Oh." Betel said as he went back to his scan of the Erne.

"I will be in my ready room, bring in the reports from the surface?"

Betel retrieved the reports and handed the data log to Voltron.

"The Zariftians are all but wiped out. A few surviving warriors were given the option to go home or to be workers on our moons. I guess you know which they chose. It was as you said; they were no match for our warriors." Betel said. "Why do you think King Zarift attacks us now knowing he could not win?"

"I am not sure." He rubbed his throbbing head. "I believed that father had sealed the deal with King Zarift, I was to mate his daughter Tess. Even though I do not love Princess Tess, I was willing to be used as such to keep our valuable gems safe." Voltron said as he shook his head. "I just don't understand it myself. You know the girl in my quarters claims to be the Princess of Zarift." He said snorting. "I know for sure she is not since Princess Tess is King Zarifts only daughter."

"You believe her to be untruthful?" asked Betel.

"Yes, maybe, I am not sure Betel." Voltron answered.

"If you need me I will be on the bridge." Betel left the ready room to continue gathering all the reports that needed the Kings review.

Scanning the reports Voltron swore shaking his head, *"Damn, the death toll was high."* Rising from his chair Voltron went to the bridge turning to Arielle, "Notify father the outcome of the skirmish. Let him know we will remain in orbit around Zephron for a month. Have ships stores bring supplies on board for the duration of our watch."

"I will be in my quarters if I am needed." Nodding he left the bridge. Once in the elevator he changed his mind instead he said "Deck 5." He was hungry and needed a good stiff drink. He needed to think.

Entering the galley he in haled deeply smiling. "Ea, what is that smell?"

Ea poked his head out of the cooking chambers grinning, "Why it is your favorite. Roast cremi. I had the supply shuttle bring it up when I heard you were injured." He slapped Voltron on the back. "I knew when you recovered you would be ravenous."

Laughing Voltron sat at the table. Ea brought his plate heaped with roast cremi, steamed tarrow root, shredded greens and his favorite bread along with a large stein of barley ale. Setting the plate in front of Voltron, he said. "Eat up my friend." He also had a large stein of barley ale as well.

"To health." Ea said as he raised his glass to salute Voltron. "Aye, Ea *to health*." He said saluting his longtime friend. He was having a nice time talking and laughing with Ea and it was many hours later when Voltron came stumbling out of the elevator and walking on wobbling legs to his door he waited till the door swished open then stepped in. The lights were dimmed and he didn't see Lyssa lying on the floor. Tripping over her he fell forward and crashed into the small table with an oath. Rolling to his backside he said, "What the hell? Why are you on the floor?" he demanded, watching her rise above him.

"I refuse to sleep in your bed." She exclaimed, crossing her arms across her chest.

Rising carefully his head felt dizzy the result of the ale. "You will sleep in my bed and you will not deny me!" he tried to sound mad but his slurred speech sounded quite less than a snarl. He lunged for her. She sidestepped his advances watching as he fell face first on to the bed. He rolling over and tried to jump up only managing to rise slowly. He grabbed at her again. She easily twirled out his grasp. With too much forward momentum, he fell head first into the cleansing chamber as the doors swished opened. Breathing heavily he rolled over. "By the gods of Zephron, Lyssa hold still so I can get you." he slurred his word.

"You will never get me again." She spoke with confidence.

"Oh . . . yes . . . I" trying to get up he fell backwards into a drunken sleep.

Laughing Lyssa jumped in the middle of the big bed hugging the pillow to her. She would be safe tonight at least the big barbarian had drunk himself silly.

The next morning Voltron woke with a splitting headache and a bad taste in his mouth. *How did I get on the floor in the cleansing chamber?* He frowned. Rising from the floor he looked in the mirror grimacing at what he saw, *why oh why did I drink all that ale?* Rinsing his face with chilled water he knew why. *Because, of that little hellion.* Stripping he returned his thoughts to Lyssa. Stepping into the stall he turned on the warm water standing there letting the water revive him. *I will never let another female that close to me again. NEVER!* "Never!" he roared. Hitting the drying button, he turned his body to let the air dry him. He stormed out of the chamber. *"I'll show her who is boss here."*

Seeing his sheets torn from the bed and wadded into a ball on the floor only ignited his anger. Looking around the room he didn't see Lyssa and his heart clenched. Rushing toward the door he turned as his eye caught a movement in the bed. Going to the bed he looked again. She was so small he hadn't even seen her there lying between the two huge pillows.

Lying down beside her he began caressing her soft skin. As he inhaled her scent he lost some of his anger toward her. Cupping her breast, he kissed her mouth letting his lips linger on her moist lips hoping she would wake up to his caresses. Rolling her over and he pushed up her shirt. Taking her nipple into his mouth, he sucked on the delicious pebble. *What is wrong with her, she is not responding to me?* Running his hand up her inner thigh, he began massaging her core placing his fingers in side her rubbing her pleasure center. He felt her lips she wasn't even wet. Moving down he placed his mouth where his fingers had been, sucking, licking and tasting her. He wanted to arouse her but nothing was happening. Pulling back he lifted his head. *Damn, what was wrong with her?* Looking up he saw her watching him indifferent to his touch. Rising above her he growled, "What have you done Lyssa?"

"Why Voltron?" she smiled taunting him "Are you not man enough to arouse me? Sitting up she looked at him, "I told you earlier that you could take me but I would never give myself to you again. I will no long take pleasure in your touch. You hate me and refuse me your love then," standing she looked him squarely in the eyes, "then I will deny you the pleasure of arousing me." Laughing she got up and dressed in his tunic. "Now, if you will take me to the training room I have waited for you long enough." She dared him to say no, and remembering she said, "You promised to take me there on your word, so is your word no good?"

she could see she was having quite an effect on him and tried not to smile.

He looked at her incredulously. *What was wrong with her?* She had responded to his touch each time he had taken her but, now nothing. Confusion washed over his face and he continued to look at her dumb founded. Rising he turned to her his arousal unquenched getting dressed he adjusted himself in his tight uniform pants. Staring intensely at her he grunted, "You are lucky I am a man of my word." Grabbing her roughly by the upper arm they left his quarters.

She worked hard exercising her body, going through the training routine. She wanted to make herself tired with all the activity. After her work out she used the training decks cleansing chambers. Going back in to the training room she watched as Voltron was still training with Biden. Sitting on the mats she laid back against the wall to watch Voltron. His muscles rippled as he trained with Biden, even though he was muscular and handsome he still needed to be taught a lesson. Biden was training as hard as Voltron. He circled Voltron slowly, watching every move Voltron made. They were holding wooden poles. Taking a swipe at Biden Voltron tripped him. Rising from the floor

Biden reached for his sword. Lyssa gasped causing Voltron to turn and seeing Biden with a sword, he dove for his.

Biden looked angry and the fighting was getting heated. Voltron was not going to backing down it was as if he still wanted to punish Biden. Lyssa sat forward fear grabbing her stomach as a pain ripped through her. Blade for blade the two warriors struck again and again. Voltron was getting tired, he wasn't completely healed and Biden was taking advantaged of Voltron's weak arm. Biden kept coming at Voltron, twisting and lunging. Biden twisted at the last minute and brought the blade down on Voltron's upper arm cutting him deep.

Screaming Lyssa jumped to action. She ran at Biden kicking his feet out from under him. Sliding across the floor she grabbed the wooden pole. Jumping up she turned and charged at him again. He stood his ground and thought he was ready for her. Standing with his feet apart knees bent he had his sword ready to swing at her. Falling on her hip she slide between his legs and forced the pole up and into his groin. Screaming with pain, Biden fell on his knees holding his groin. From another area of the training room, Betel and Arthur heard

Biden's scream and ran into the training room. When they saw all the blood and Lyssa standing over Biden with a wooden pole they rushed forward and grabbed her arms. "Hey!" she said as they removed the pole from her hand.

Rising to his feet Voltron yelled. "Halt. She has done nothing wrong." They released her and went to Voltron. "Commander you are covered with blood." Arthur spoke trying to see where the blood was coming from. Taking off his belt he saw the deep gash in Voltron's upper left arm. "Let me bind you before you bleed to death."

"What happened here?" Betel asked clearly angry to find his friend hurt yet again.

"Biden became overzealous in our match. He twisted and swung the blade hitting me in the arm. Lyssa then jumped up and took him out with the wooden pole. Please check on him as I think he may be ruined for life." Voltron said, as all eyes went to her as she turned crimson.

Clearing her throat she spoke, "I was unsure of what to do I just didn't want Biden injuring you again. I am sorry if I damaged him for life." She couldn't help the smirk of her face.

"I will take him to sick bay." Lyssa said. Betel looked at her and spoke, "Which one?"

"I will take Voltron to sick bay. Betel will you please tend to Biden I am sure he doesn't want me near him right now." She turned to see that Biden still holding his groin rolling around on the floor. Turning she took Voltron's good arm and placed it over her shoulder putting her arm around his waist. It was quite comical, he so tall and she so small. He was amazed at her strength for as small as she was she took as much of his weight as he would allow.

Entering sick bay Lyssa smiled at Belgorod. "What do we have here?" he asked.

"Biden was overzealous in his training my arm took the brunt of his eagerness." Voltron sat down on the medical bed.

"I will take it from here if you wish to return to Voltron's quarter Lyssa." Belgorod took the healing unit out of the drawer. "Are your headaches getting better?" he inquired.

"Yes, yes they are thanks for asking. Yes, I think I will return I am very tired. Good night to you both." she turned and left.

"I am glad she left we need to talk." Belgorod spoke severely to Voltron. Voltron raised his eyebrow at the Belgorod's tone.

"You sound as if you are angry we with me?"

"I am." He hesitated for a brief minute before he launch into Voltron. "I have noticed that Lyssa seems to be crying a lot lately." Clearing his throat he went on, "I went to your quarters the other day to give her some pills for her headaches and found her curled in a ball on your floor. It was clear she had been crying. Her eyes were red and puffy."

Taking off his viewing devise he looked straight into Voltron's eyes. "If you are abusing her Voltron I swear I will bring it up with your father. She has done nothing so severe to you that you should treat her unfairly. Remember you are a prince of Zephron and as Zephron's prince you need to up hold the law. Do I need to quote the law to you Voltron?" Placing his hands on his hips he waited for Voltron's response.

Voltron thought of Belgorod as an uncle to him. It seemed that the healer had taken a liking to Lyssa. Turning crimson he spoke softly to Belgorod, "I have been harsh with my words I will admit that but it is because she thinks I should love her just because I mounted her."

Slamming his fist down on the cart Belgorod looked at Voltron. "You have mated with her?" his voice rose. "Why in the names of the gods and goddesses did you mount her when you had no intentions of loving her? You do not want another mate yet you take her, mount her and then make her suffer for your mistakes. Does she know that by the simple act of mating with you that you are bound for life?" he asked incredulously.

Rising from the medical bed he looked at Belgorod, "Have a care Belgorod you over step your bounds. I take her because she eases my loneliness but I will not love her. I do not abuse her. I know very well what the law says about abusing woman."

Sighing Belgorod pushed at him to sit on the med bed so he could finish with the healing units cycle. Looking at Voltron's arm he was satisfied that the slight scar would heal completely in a couple of days. "I do not understand you Voltron. I know Elena hurt you more than you let on and in that hurt I find you hurting others. All I am saying is don't harm her Voltron take care with her."

"I am not abusive to her I did not use her without her understanding where I stood. I simply will not love. Are we done?" he said harshly as he rose to leave.

"Yes." Belgorod turned away from his Prince and commander.

"Then I shall return to my quarters." He strode from the sick bay angry at Lyssa and why he couldn't put his finger on it.

In his quarters Lyssa was in the cleansing chamber brushing her long golden hair. Taking the sleeping shirt from the drawer she slipped the material over her head. Turning to leave she started as Voltron stood in the door watching her. She was trying to judge his mood but he was sometimes unreadable.

Softening his feature he spoke, "Thank you for coming to my aide." He smiled at her. "I didn't realize you cared for me that much." He said raising his eyebrows at her as she turned pink.

"Um, I, well . . . I thought you were injured worse than you were. If I had known it was but a flesh wound, I would not have attacked poor Biden." Smiling she looked at him with beautiful sea green eyes that sparkled. "I take it Biden is alright?" she questioned.

"Yes Belgorod made sure he was not any more pain. However, he may be walking a little strange for a day or two." Walking toward her he bent to kiss her. Teasing her lips with his tongue he waited for her to open her mouth. When she did not respond to his kiss he tired caressing her breast. He then pulled her legs up around his waist pressing her sex against his hard shaft as he lowered his head to inhale her scent. She was motionless in his arms and his anger flared with in him. Dropping her quickly she almost fell to the floor. Pushing her up against the wall he hit the wall next to her head glaring at her, "how are you doing this you little witch?

Turning innocent eyes upon him she asked, "What do you think I am doing?" she asked so sweetly.

"Do not mess with me Lyssa. I know I have not lost my touch to arouse you so you must be doing something that allows you to not respond to my touches!"

Walking away from him, "I have no idea what you are inferring Voltron. I told you that since you do not love me that I would no longer respond to your touch. Did you doubt me?" She asked raising her eyebrows at him.

Grabbing her by the shoulders he shook her, "Then I will take you rather you enjoy it or not." Lifting her roughly in his arms he stormed to the bed. Ripping her clothes off he stood and looked at her full round breast, her soft skin. Letting his eyes room down her body his breathing quickened.

Inhaling deeply he wanted to smell her arousal, he wanted her to want him and damn she didn't want him. Falling down on the bed beside her he grabbed her kissing her roughly. She did not raise her arms to pull him down on her. He roughly placed his hand on her sex and sought her channel with his fingers. Inserting his fingers and finding her dry he swore again. "Damn you," he cursed. Raising his fist he hit the bed beside her, growling. Jumping up he stormed from her presences.

Tears burned behind her eye lids. She felt bad at what she was doing to him. *He has to learn a lesson he cannot expect me to fall into his arms willingly knowing I will never be loved by him.* Brushing away her tears with the back of her hand she rose and went into the chamber and got another shirt to sleep in. Returning to the bed she looked at it longingly, even though the pills made her unresponsive to Voltron's caresses she still wanted him. *Maybe I should stop taking the medicine and let him have his way. I miss him. I don't want to love him if he can't love me back. Damn Elena you damaged a great warrior and lover.* Deciding the bed was too big without Voltron's presences she grabbed the pillow and the covering and walked around the bed to lay on the floor.

It was in the middle of the fourth watch that Voltron finally stumbled into his quarters. Sitting on the bed he tore off his shirt. Standing he tried to undress but he was having trouble because of all the ale he had drank. Sitting back down on the bed he reached down to take off his boots once he had them off he lifted legs to lie on the bed. Lying there, he tied recalled how Lyssa had jumped to his defense. "Lyssa, my Lyssa you are so beautiful. I want to love you but I just cannot. Why can't you just make love to me? Why do I have to love you? I cannot be hurt again, I don't think my heart could take it, please just let me mount you." Rolling over he tried to sleep.

Voltron had awakened Lyssa when he came in; she rose up to see what he was doing. He looked so tired he was having trouble taking off his clothes. She silently watched him as he struggled to take off his pants. She was about to get up and help when he declared his need for her. Her heart tightened. Hearing the anguish in his voice her heart broke making a decision she thought, *I will stop taking the medicine. It wasn't his fault that his heart was broken by his unfaithful mate.* Rising from the floor, she went to him and lay down beside him on the bed.

At first, he was confused as he felt her lay down. She slowly turned him over so she could kiss him. Unbuttoning his shirt she kissed his neck then trailed her kisses down to his chest licking one of his nipples. He groaned and looked up. "Lyssa don't start something you can't finish." He spoke through clenched teeth.

Unbuttoning his pants she placed her hand on his hot shaft and rubbed it up and down. Seeing a pearl size drop of fluid coming from his slit, she bent and tasted it with her tongue. He tasted sweet. Grabbing her he brought her up and rolled her over kissing her.

She held him close speaking softly to him, "I am so sorry Voltron that Elena hurt you. It was not me that harmed you breaking your heart it was her, yet you take your hurt and anger out on me and I can't let you do that." She paused hoping he understood where she was coming from.

He stopped his advances and turned on his back. He didn't pull her into his arms he just laid there. Soon she heard his even breathing; she knew he had fallen to sleep. She pulled the covers up and placed then on him. Bending she brushed a stray lock of his hair off his for head. Looking down at him she had to admit he was the most handsome man she had ever seen. She longed to be in his arms and after tomorrow she would be. No more games she would let him take her and then she would form a plan to make him fall in love with her.

She rose early, went to Belgorod, and explained what the pills were really used for and her shame at having used them to get even with Voltron. She needed a her blood scanned to see just how much of the drug was left in her system.

Laughing Belgorod smiled at her, "Well my dear someone had to teach the mean warrior a thing or two. I am sure he is wondering why he can't arouse you but it will be our little secret." Ok he nodded. Rising on her tip toes she kissed him on the cheek. Turning she left sick bay to go back to Voltron's quarters.

Entering his quarters she found him still sleeping, she went and took a shower. Afterwards she was brushing her long hair when she heard him stir. She had dressed in a short tunic of his, since her clothes where in short supply. She would just have to keep wearing his shirts or sleeping shirts.

He was trying to get up when she remembered he had left his pants down around his ankles.

Going to him she pulled them off and stood before him looking at him, letting her eyes trail down his frame to his arousal. Pulling the sheet off him completely, she kneeled on the floor between his legs. Picking up his shaft she massaged it and kissed it until she heard him groaning. Taking the tunic off her, she rose above him and lowered herself onto his shaft. Looking at her he was amazed at her boldness. Rising up and down she leaned forward to kiss him. Mesmerized by her actions, and he was not sure if this were a dream or real. Reaching up he took breasts and rubbed. Leaning up he took her nipple in his mouth and even though the medicine had yet to wear off, she never let him know.

She continued her riding of him and soon he was caught up on the rhythm of her movements. Voltron rolled them over so he could thrust deeper into her sheath. All the time kissing her lips, *Oh Voltron I will make you love me just you wait and see.* His release was near and she felt him bury himself deep within her body, he nuzzled her neck again and bit down as his release shook him to the core. He lay on her gently kissing her face. "I knew you could not resist me Lyssa." He spoke with confidence.

Rolling from him she got off the bed put her tunic on and stared at him lying on his side watching her. Placing her hands on her hips she spoke, "Do not be so sure Voltron, you did not hear me cry out your name did you?" She asked raising an eyebrow. Turning she went to the food panel and hit the button for hot tea. Taking the cup she went to the table and sat down to sip her tea. He looked at her with anger again in his eyes. Rising he went to the cleansing chamber and dressed. Hitting the food panel he ordered hot grog, taking it he sat down beside her. Sighing heavily he spoke, "I am tired of fighting with you Lyssa."

She looked at him and said, "Then don't be so mean to me. The only time I have ever hurt you was when I attacked you during the skirmish. Yet you attack me on a daily basis, you do not really want me for a mate yet you said you would mate me but I would never be loved. I cannot live like that Voltron, for I have had nothing but love and acceptance my whole life, first from my parents and then from the warrior's I command. Maybe you have shut your heart off to love but I have not." Rising she put her cup in the sanitary unit and went to the door. Turning she spoke again. "I am going to the training deck Arthur has ordered me a training garment. Will come with me or will you stay?" when he didn't answer she left.

Who does she think she is talking to? I have had love as well my parents love me and my brothers, even Elena had loved me at first, or at least I thought she had. She is not the only one who can't live without love. Slamming the grog down, he rose then left his quarters to follow her. *She knows it angers me when she goes about the ship without a guard.*

She had barely gotten to the transport elevator when Voltron's big hand reached over her and pushed the open panel. Inside he spoke, "Deck 7." Once on the training deck Lyssa saw Arthur training another young warrior. She went to him without Voltron by her side. Smiling she waved at him. Stopping his training he went to the bench near the wall and picked up a package. Smiling he brought it to her. "Here are the training clothes I promised you." he said.

Taking the package from him she ripped open the paper and took out the slacks and the tunic that she would wear when training. Hugging them to her she raised on her tip toes to kiss Arthur's cheek. "Awe lass," he spoke his cheeks turning red.

She turned to show Voltron what Arthur had gotten her and she was met with angry eyes. Rolling hers she ignored him. Going to the cleansing chamber she put on her new outfit. Coming out she did a small twirl to show Arthur how nice the garments fit. "Can I train with you today warrior Arthur?" she asked sweetly as she bowed.

"Sure lass, this here is Colton he be one of our youngest warrior's we were just practicing some of the maneuvers we have seen you do. Would you mind showing him how they are done?"

Glowing with pride that Arthur would want her to show his warriors some of her training maneuver she quickly went to Colton shaking his hand. "Just because I am female Colton you are not to hold back. I will show you the moves and then we will spar." She took the wooden shaft and stood side by side with Colton showing him her spinning jump kick, then her running slid that she had used on Biden. Twisting, turning and jumping at the last second were just some of her moves. Soon Biden and several other young warriors were watching as she trained Colton. Turning to the group she said, "Pick up your shafts and attack Colton and I." Grabbing their shafts they began circling her and Colton as he stood at Lyssa's back.

When Biden swung out with his pole she ducked and brought her pole up and knocked him in the chest, just as Colton swung and hit him in the side knocking him off his feet. Veltrain charged at them both with the wooden shaft horizontal, Lyssa dropped missing his pole swinging her pole up and jarring his wooden pole loose. Jumping up she used her spinning kick and hit Veltrain square in the side of his head with her foot. Colton spun taking Connor's feet out from under him. Adair started to attack and then thought better of it as he saw his companions lying on the floor. Lyssa and Colton stood in their midst. Patting her on the back Colton picked her up and spun her around giving out a war cry of victory. Rising from the mat the other warriors bowed to her and then clapped her on the back as well.

Looking at her as she sparred with his men made him smile. His heart swelled in his chest as he watched her put three of his men down, but when Colton picked her up and spun her around he growled out his disapproval. Colton had dropped her quickly when he heard the growl. The last thing he wanted was to anger his commander.

Going to her side Voltron put his arm around her protectively. Arthur stood by and smiled at

Voltron. "She is as good a fighter as any of our men." He said with pride.

"Yes she is but from now on I will be the one training with her."

Hearing this, his men all groaned with disappointment. Turning to his men he spoke calmly, "She is mine, no other will touch her. Do I make myself clear?"

Pulling away from him she looked up at him angrily spinning around she left the training deck not waiting for him. *He was so infuriating I would like to knock him over the head with one of those wooden shafts except he would probably pass out.* Pressing the transport panel she hit Deck 4. Going to his room she removed her training clothes and placed them in the cleaning tube. Showering she was just drying off when he stormed into the chamber.

"Lyssa, you are not to wander the decks alone without me, Betel or Arthur."

"I am a big girl Voltron I do not need your protection. Surely you must know by now watching me in training that I can protect myself."

Going to her he picked up a lock of her golden hair smelling it as he did. "You always smell so nice." She leaned into him liking the feel of him so near. "Why must we always fight?" he asked softly.

"It is not my wish to fight with you Voltron." She said but she felt dizzy and swayed a little. Concerned he picked her up and took her to the bed. Laying her down he looked at her and asked if she needed the healer to come. "No Voltron I am fine I am just tired." Lying down beside her he covered her with the covers and held her close.

She lay in his arms snuggled close to his chest. Breathing in his scent she sighed. "I love you I love you so much why can't you love me?" she said softly as she drifted off to sleep.

Hearing her soft voice declaring her love for him made him hold her closer. Caressing her hair, he spoke soothingly to her as she continued to sleep. *She was on the training deck watching Voltron and Biden fighting, she felt sick to her stomach something bad was going to happen to her Voltron. Rising she screamed out his name. Then she saw the sword come down and pierce his heart. As his blood flowed from his body, she cried out.* Waking she was cold and sweating looking around in the darkness she saw Voltron rise on his knees and take her gently into his arms. Calming her heart she pushed against him, "I am alright." Voltron looked at her his face softened as he realized she loved him. Lying back down, he pulled her to him. "What were you dreaming about Lyssa?" he asked softly.

"I thought you were killed when Biden attacked you." she replied quietly. Pulling her even closer he spoke, "I am here my love. I am not going away."

She almost stopped breathing did he call her his love? Not caring if he meant it or not just for tonight she would revel in the thought that perhaps he did or could love her. Nestled in his arms she fell asleep again this time resting easier than before.

Voltron was gone when she woke the next morning. Rolling over she rub the placed that he had been lying wishing that he hadn't left her so soon. Getting up she felt dizzy again and now her stomach felt sick. What was going on, had she caught something. Lying back down she felt a little better and decided that maybe today she would just rest.

It was well passed the midday watch when Voltron had called Betel into his ready room. "Come in Betel." Voltron motioned for him to take a seat. Rising Voltron hit the food panel button and ordered two grogs. Handing Betel a glass he asked, "How long have we been friend's Betel?"

"Most of our lives, why do you ask" Betel wondered what was going through Voltron's head.

"Most of our lives, would you say I have been a fair man, a man of honor and integrity?" he asked looking out the window of his starship barely noticing the universe pass by.

"I would say that for most of your life yes you have been a good, honest, fair man with integrity." Betel took a sip of the grog.

Hearing the hesitation in Betel Voltron asked again, "Are you sure, if I have not been tell me."

"You have always been a fair man, but lately you seem preoccupied by Lyssa. Whenever she is near you seem angry and unsettled. The incident in the galley took a lot of the men by surprise especially when you have made it known that you do not care for Lyssa." Downing his drink he rose and went to Voltron. "You know your actions do not match your eyes I think you are in love with her but you will not allow it because of Elena." Placing his hand on Voltron's shoulder he went on. "I know how deeply you were hurt, but other than the physical wound she gave you during a battle Lyssa has done nothing to you except get into your heart. Am I right Voltron?"

Downing his drink he went to desk and sat down, "Yes you are right. I did not want to love her. I did not want to care for here. I should have never mounted her from that moment on my heart has been in turmoil."

"If you love her Voltron then mate her."

"You know, I even bit her on the neck." He said shaking his head.

"You what!" exclaimed Betel. "Then surely you must know that she is carrying your seed. You can't let her training anymore and you need to take better care of her." Betel said a little angry at his friend. "You know that our bit brings the womb of a female to fertility fast. Has she shown any signs of pregnancy he asked?"

"No, but last evening in the cleansing chamber she became dizzy and she looked pale." He said softly.

"Then you must have her see Belgorod."

"When the time is right I will. Until then I am going to do the mating ritual with her and bind her to me heart and soul."

Smiling Betel jumped up and slapped his friend on the shoulder. "Well done Voltron. You won't be sorry." He left.

His time on the bridge had gone quickly. Voltron gave orders to com him if they needed and left to go to his quarters. He planned on getting food and then explaining to Lyssa that he would mate with her. He would eventually learn to love her. Of course he wouldn't tell her that.

Entering his quarters he went to his bedroom to change out of his uniform. He noticed that Lyssa was still in bed sound asleep. Going to her he woke her gently. "Are you alright Lyssa?"

Groaning she shook her head yes. "Don't move the bed I feel nauseated."

"Do you want me to call Belgorod?"

"No just let me sleep I will be fine in the morning." Rolling over she went back to sleep.

I guess I'll wait till tomorrow to perform the mating ritual he thought. Going to the food panel he punched in a container with water. Placing the Oprhys tenthredinifera, a large purple flower that grew on Zephron, in the container he would wait and give it to her tomorrow. He had ordered it this morning when he had made the decision to mate her. He was in luck as the supply ship was just leaving. He wanted to give her something beautiful from Zephron so that she knew he was going to try and love her.

Undressing he crawled in bed beside her holding her gently caressing her hair. It was the middle of the sleep cycle when Voltron woke to her pushing several buttons on the food panel. Rising he went to her and asked, "What are you doing?" Turning to him she had a piece of meat hanging out of her mouth and was about to take a plate of steamed vegetables out of the food panel. He looked down at her with a shocked expression, "Are you hungry now?" he asked.

Smiling she shook her head yes, sitting the plate of vegetables on the table she took the meat out of her mouth. "I am starving. Are you hungry?" she asked offering a piece of meat.

"You were sick when I came in from my shift, now you are hungry?"

"Yes, I feel like I haven't eaten in days." Turning she grab an eating utensil and sat at the round table and began eating the plate of food.

"Hum that does smell good. I didn't eat after my watch so maybe I will join you." Going to the food panel he punched in a few buttons and a hot steaming plate of vegetables and meat came out. Inhaling deeply he smiled at her "Yes I am hungry, sure smells good."

They talked and visited while they ate their late night meal. After they were done Voltron took her hand and led her back to their bed. Sitting on the bed with her he smiled at her. "I want to do the binding ritual with you. Will you allow me to?" he asked uncertain if she would let him.

Her heart skipped a beat he wanted to mate with her for life, if the binding ritual was preformed then they would be bound for an eternity. No one could break this ritual except them. They could break it by leaving the other or if the other died. It was a beautiful ritual one she had always wanted with her mate. There was still the question though of his love. Could she bind to a man who may never love her? If she didn't mate with this man then there really was no chance in her mating with anyone else since her purity had been taken by him. Chewing on her lower lip she was trying to take it all in when Voltron let out a long sigh. She looked up to see that he had a tic in his jaw. She knew he was upset because she hadn't answered right away.

Clearing her throat she placed her hand on his arm, "I will do the bind ritual with you Voltron. I will do it knowing you will never love me like you loved Elena. If it is all you have to offer me then I accept your offer."

Looking down at her he knew what she said was hurting her. He couldn't promise love all he could promise was protection, care and a mate for life. He wanted to offer her more but he just didn't trust her enough to let his heart lover her. Picking up her hand he raised it to his lips and kissed the palm. "Then let us proceed. Will you undress and kneel before me?"

They both knelt naked in front of each other. He took her hands and bowed his head. She followed his lead. "May the gods and goddesses of Zephron unite us together heart, soul, mind and body. With all that I am I willingly pledge to protect you, take care of you and give you many babies to make our life together happy. You repeat after me now Lyssa." She said the vows with a heaviness of heart, she knew he had purposefully left out the "to love part".

Pulling her toward him he sealed their binding ritual with a kiss. She eagerly kissed him back, kissing him deeply, pushing her naked breasts into his chest. When they parted it was he who was breathless. Smiling she reached up and kissed each eye then pushed him down on the bed.

Lying down beside him she laid her head on his shoulder. The food had sated her stomach and the ritual part of her heart now with his warmth beside her she felt tired again and allowed the peaceful feeling to loll her asleep.

Voltron laid there trying to quite his trembling heart. He wanted her so badly but she was already asleep again. Smiling to himself he thought, *I will let you sleep for now but in the morning we will seal the binding with our bodies.*

CHAPTER THREE

Sister or Foe

*P*rincess Tess ran her hand over the beautiful crystal like gem that she had gotten from the Calum. Placing the gem next to her face it felt cold and hard just like her heart she smiled. Sneering she thought, *I will not marry Prince Voltron no matter what my father bargained for. I just proved to myself that I don't need a marriage agreement to obtain the gems.* Taken from her revere by a pounding on her door she yelled, "Who is it? Who in the blazes is bothering me now?"

"Begging your pardon Princess," the warrior Calum bowed before her.

"Yes, what is it Calum?"

"You have lost the battle on Zephron." He spoke quietly, "Most of your Warriors are either dead or missing." Gulping he bowed his head, "You even lost your sister Lyssa." He said sadly.

Rising and throwing the gem at Calum, she stared down at him. "What are we to do now Calum? Do you think I care one wit that my stupid little sister is missing or may even be dead? Do YOU?" she screamed. "All I care about is the fact that you did not penetrate their city to kill King Zephron. Do you not understand that I will not marry his stupid son Prince Voltron! I don't give a damn about an alliance with them in order to gain access to the gem." turning swiftly she strode to the window. "Does my father know that Lyssa is missing?"

"No my lady, we have not informed him yet. We did have word though it was thought that Prince Voltron is the one who captured her." He said his head still bowed.

"Um, interesting," she said with an evil smile. Turning back to him she spoke, "You will gather, Warriors Boden and Vaughn and meet me at my country house in seven days. There we shall plot the destruction of King Zephron and his sons." Sneering at Calum she continued, "Then we will be in charge of the gems and the technology to use it. Once I am in control of the gems my father will not be able to make me marry him or any one. Now hurry do my bidding before I have the Warrior of the guards take you prisoner." She laughed evilly.

"As you wish my Princess," Bowing low Calum rose swiftly and left, fuming inside at her wickedness. He had no choice though but to do her biding, if the King ever found out that he had taken liberties with her he would hang on the gallows for all to see his shame.

It had been several days since King Zarift had heard anything regarding Lyssa. He paced back and forth in front of the fire place, his thoughts on his youngest daughter. Zephorah watched as her husband paced relentlessly, she watched as each expression moved across his face. She knew he was angry with himself for letting Lyssa be in charge of the warriors, even though Zariftian law stated that the second child male or female, of the King would rule over the warrior class.

"My love, come and sit by me and drink your grog. It will help you relax." She said lifting the glass to him. Turning he walked toward her, she was the most beautiful woman he had ever seen and he thanked the gods and goddesses that she was his. He softened his expression and sighed deeply.

"Aye, Zephorah, I will come and sit for a while," he sat next to her. Lifting the glass of grog to his lips, he drank. "I blame myself for Lyssa being captured." Making a fist he slammed it down on his thigh. "And to think Prince Voltron is the one to take her. I promised him Tess but no he had to have my youngest." He slammed the glass down so hard that Zephorah thought it would break.

"You cannot blame yourself for the law. It has been a law for thousands and thousands a years. Lyssa should have been a son." Zephorah said sadly. "If I had given you a son then there would have been no problem. He would have ruled the Warrior class well." She swiped at a tear as it ran down her cheek.

Going to her Zarift knelt down beside her. "I love Lyssa, and she has been the joy of my life. You gave her to me and replaced the heartache I have felt all these years in Tess. My first wife hated me when she bore a daughter for me she killed herself." Disgust in his voice, "I have tried all that I knew how to do to love Tess but she has her mother's hatred for me and my kingdom."

"I know, I know, Zarift, you have tried everything to make her love you."

Zarift walked to the window, the sunset was beautiful, the kind that Lyssa would have sat and watched as she played her harp and sang her songs. "What I don't know is why Prince Voltron has not made his demand known? Does he think he can just keep Lyssa without retribution?"

"I do not know my husband. Perhaps you should try and communicate with King Zephron again. May be this time the message will reach him and not one of his Warriors." Zephorah rose, "I am tired, will you join me my chambers?" she asked smiling lovingly at him.

His heart melted. Walking to her he took her hand as they walked to her bed chambers.

Sitting in her chair drinking the grog she leered at Boden. "It took you long enough to get here!" exclaimed Tess.

"Indeed my lady, but we wanted to make sure no one would follow us." Boden said.

"We are here now my lady, what is your plan?" Calum asked bitterly.

"My plan is that we kill Prince Voltron, the king and my stupid little sister. But of course we will need to make it look like an accident." Her eyes narrowed to slits.

"How will we get them all in one place?" asked Vaughn.

"My plan is simple; really, in four months the galactic council will be meeting for the *Athnam* to review galactic laws. Prince Voltron, King Zephron and my father will be in attendance." She spoke swirling her drink.

"What about Princess Lyssa." Calum asked.

"I am sure if Voltron captured her he will bring her with him. Maybe he will try and ransom her back to my father." Taking a big gulp of the grog, she smiled. "We will just have to make sure that they are all together when we kill them at the *Athnam*." She grinned brazenly.

"What?" stormed Boden and Vaughn together.

"You can't be serious?" Calum ask incredulously.

Jumping to her feet she slammed the glass down violently on the table. "I can and I will." She grinned evilly, "Why it is shear genius. We will kill all of them and no one will know who is behind the attack. We can turn to our allies and continue the war with Zephron."

"No one will follow us into a full scale galactic war!" stormed Calum, "You must be mad!"

Rushing at him she got in his face, "I'll show you madness, how mad will you be after I tell my father what you did to me?" she snarled. "He may not love me as much as his precious little Lyssa," she spat out. "But he will not tolerate that kind of behavior among his warriors." Turning toward the other two she spoke very slowly, looking straight into their eyes, "You will meet with our allies to seek their help or you will all die. Do I make myself clear?"

Storming from the house Calum spoke softly to the two, "I don't know about you but I am not going to get killed because of one crazy female."

"What are we going to do if we don't do what she asked of us?" Boden asked fear clearly in his words.

"Stop sniveling like a *bantling*." Vaughn said. "You are a warrior, act like one."

"Calum what is your plan?" Vaughn asked, hoping Calum had a better plan than that stupid fey back there."

"We are all warrior spies on Commander Tiernan's ship, they will be returning to Varian within one month. I heard from Chief Communication officer Arlana that, Prince Voltron's ship the Erne will be on Varian seven days after that, Lyssa should be on the Erne," he paused for effect.

"Yes?" Both warriors said, "Then what?" Vaughn continued.

"We blast the base command center in the confusion we will go to Voltron's quarters and take Lyssa. We will then bring her back to King Zarift. He will be so thankful that he will richly reward us. Once we have the *dinars* we leave Zarift and Zephron far behind."

"What of Princess Tess?" Boden asked.

"What of her?" Calum stormed, "If you want to take your chances with her then go right ahead. Go back to her. As for me I will not, she is evil. I wish I had known when I had taken liberties with her."

"Well Boden?" Vaughn asked, "Where does your loyalty lie, with us or with her?"

"With you my friends with you."

Killian waited till the Warriors had left. Walking up behind her he put his arms around her waist, "You seem upset my dear." Kissing her neck his hand went up her bodice and cupped her breast. Turning in his arms she kissed him deeply.

"I love you Killian, I will not marry this Prince Voltron. We will kill him and his father and hopefully my bitch of a sister. When we do Killian, you will become my mate and we will live together with the power of the gems in our hands." She laughed. Leaning into him she placed a hand upon his hard shaft, "Take me Killian make me yours. Plant your seed deep within me. I will do anything to shame my father."

He stiffened at her request. "You would only want my seed so you can shame your father, Tess?" Pulling away from her he turned his back on her, "I am not one to give away something as dear to me as my offspring's, if you could not love my child then there would be no point in giving you my seed. Do I make myself clear Tess?"

Going to him she stood on her toes snuggling against him. "My love, I did not mean it that way." She lied so easily. "I meant with your seed deep inside me, and my belly growing with your love. My father will die of a brain seizure." She cackled. "I will be very happy to have your child." She cooed. "I will love it as much as I love you." She hid the disgust showing on her face by turning in his arms lifting her hair for him to kiss her neck.

"You are so evil my Tess. But then again that is what I love about you." he smirked behind her back. *She was not the only one who had plans for their future. I wanted to be King and by marrying Tess I can be once we rid ourselves of that little trollop Lyssa.* Smiling cruelly he pondered his takeover of Zarift

The Erne had arrived back at Varian seven days ago. Sitting at the console Voltron continued to drum fingers. It had been many days since the attack from the Zarifts. Deep in thought Voltron did not hear his younger brother come in.

Clearing his throat Tiernan stood in the door of the command center.

"Tiernan, it is good to see you my brother."

"It is good to see you Voltron. Father says he hopes all is well with you. Is it my brother?" he asked scrutinizing Voltron.

Nodding yes, he spoke "You have been with father then? Does he or the Security council have any word on why the Zarifts attacked us?" he asked

"No the Galactic Security Council is in the dark just as we are as too why the Zarifts attacked us and took our gems, especially in the face of the marriage alliance between our two worlds. There was one communications from King of Xantha. He had heard that Princess Tess did not want to marry but was doing so as an honor bound duty." Sitting in the chair, next Voltron Tiernan went on "Arlana and I spoke we thought perhaps somehow Zariftian spies came into our midst. The other thought was perhaps someone paid our own people well to betray us. It would best if we did not openly talk around the crew," he replied.

Tiernan commanded his own battle starship with his own handpicked crew. Tiernan was the battalion leader on war tactic. He gathered Intel from other planets a valuable resource for the Zephronian Warriors and the Galactic Council sought after Tiernan's vast knowledge of such. "I am here for one day and then I will be returning to the ruling council of the Athnam they have asked me to help them with security Intel.

"Will you be returning to us before we embark on our trek to the Athnam?"

"Yes I will not have to go as far as Barax; the Council is on another undisclosed location to prepare for the Athnam. I should be returning in a few days."

"Since you are here for one day will you dine with me tonight?" Voltron asked smiling at his younger brother.

"I suppose I could be convinced to dine with you if you promise to feed me your famous roast cremi?" he asked hopefully.

Rising from the console he slapped his brother on the back, "Good I will leave now to prepare it, come when you are done." He stared for the door turning, "By the way I have a female that I have taken as a mate so don't be surprised."

Tiernan raised a quizzical eyebrow.

My family will be extremely happy now that I have taken a mate. He can't wait till Tiernan meets her tonight. Sighing he thought of Lyssa waiting in his quarters, he had been happy these past weeks. *I love mounting her the way she makes me feel. Maybe after Tiernan leaves tonight I will take her again.* His steps quickened as he hurried to the tram that would take him to his quarters. *I will cook the roast cremi while waiting for Tiernan and his good company. But first I need to speak with Lyssa letting her know my younger brother will be coming for the evening meal.* He smiled as he jumped on the tram.

"Brother you make the best roast cremi this side of the Zephron." Laughing Tiernan sloshed down another drink of grog.

"You have been away too long on your mission if you think my roast cremi is so good." Voltron smiled back, downing his own grog.

"Well maybe but this is very good." Nodding to Lyssa he asked, "Don't you think it is good, my lady."

Lyssa was a little tense at meeting Voltron's brother and she was not feeling well. She felt edgy and about to explode. She grimaced at Tiernan's questions as she scowled at him.

"What have you done to her Voltron? She is so beautiful yet so angry."

Setting his grog down he spoke "I have done nothing to her, tis her nature to be contrary at times."

Glaring at him yet speaking very calmly, she responded to Voltron's comment, "I am not contrary Voltron, I am just unloved, after all you have taken me as your mate yet you will not love me as such." Lyssa concentrated on cutting her meat. Taking a bite she looked to Tiernan. "Your brother has mated me over and over again. Yet I am told he will never love me while being his mate. Even if I should carry his seed he has told me the babe will not be mine to raise. Should I be happy about this Tiernan? Pray tell me what you think?" Bitterness filled her words as she slammed her eating utensils down on the table.

"Lyssa!" Voltron roared, "Take care what you say. My brother has no need to know my business. My family understands the reason I do not love."

Watching the two of them spar was slightly amusing and frustrating. It was apparent to Tiernan that they both loved each but they were both clearly stubborn people. Clearing his throat Tiernan spoke to his brother, "I am not so sure we do understand Voltron? It is clear here that you have been abusing this beautiful woman and for that my brother I am not proud of you." Looking at the pain in Lyssa's eyes, he was angry and ashamed of his brother.

"Do not take her side Tiernan. I have explained to her that I could not love her. She has overstepped her bounds. I take her because she pleases me in bed and I have mated her, why does there have to be love? I will never love her or any other female again." Voltron glared at his brother.

"I do not understand." Tiernan said. "Elena has hurt you deeply and in doing so has not allowed you to find love with another. Father said that after he had annulled your marriage to Elena that you needed to find someone to mate to produce male heirs. He had hoped in that mating you would find love as well." Lyssa's head quickly turned to Tiernan as he spoke those words.

"Damn you Tiernan!" Voltron stormed "I will not love another, I have taken her as my mate and that is all I am willing to do. Now leave my quarters. I am through talking."

Tiernan rose quietly lifting Lyssa's hand he kissed it. "I am so sorry Lyssa; if you had known him as I did before Elena hurt him you would have loved him." With that Tiernan left.

I do love him but he does not love me her mind screamed as tears came to her eyes.

Voltron rose and stormed into his room.

Tears started again. *I wish I could have known him. I already love him but he does not love me. He is in love with a woman who has scorned him.* Lyssa cleared the table and put the food in the cooling chamber. *Why am I crying? I never cried like this before.* Tears continued to flow down her cheeks. *If I could gain his trust and show him how different Elena and I are maybe he could love me then. Or maybe Voltron couldn't love again. I know his heart was torn into by Elena but I would love him and care for him never hurting him.* A fresh sob came from her as more tears ran down her face. She turned out the lights and sought her own bed. She had asked for a different room when they had landed on Varian. She had been so sick lately that she had not wanted to keep Voltron awake with her illness. He did not seem to mind her sleeping in another room and so she resigned herself to the long lonely nights without him. She could not understand why she was ill and so very tired. She should not be since she had stopped taking the *rugart* pill.

In his room Voltron slammed his door. Swearing he pace angrily around the room. *How dare she? Speaking to my family as if they were her allies and not mine,* going to the side board he got the grog out and pour a large glass full and drained it in one drink, *and to think my brother would turn on me like that.* Pouring another glass full he drank it down again in one swallow. *Why couldn't they understand how much Elena had hurt him by leaving him with one of his own warriors? Her betrayal was harsh and still to fresh for him.* Pouring another large glass of grog Voltron drained it again. The effects of the alcohol began taking its toll on him.

He staggered toward the bed, sitting he started undressed. *Females damn they made him angry. Why did they have to be so soft so tender. I loved Elena with all of my heart.* Unbuttoning his shirt, *from the moment my father had introduced her as my mate, I loved her. I had thought she loved me. Well that's what I get for thinking.* Standing he took the glass back to the side board deciding one more drink wouldn't hurt pouring the grog he drank it down quickly, making a decision to go to Lyssa. *I have left her alone too long it is time to put her back in my bed where she belongs. I will not love her but she is my mate I will mount her as many times as I want.* Sounding like a petulant child, "Do you understand that Lyssa?" he slurred his words. Turning from his room he stumbled across the hall to her room where he barged in not bothering to knock.

Startled as her door swung open Lyssa quickly dived for her sheets. "How dare you come in here without knocking?" She stormed.

Leaning against the doorframe to steady himself he spoke his words slurred, "I don't have to knock in my own home Ly s s a!" he hiccupped.

Noticing the desire in his eyes she let her eyes trail down his nude body to the very evidence of his desire. "I shall have you Lyssa; I have neglected you for too long now." He walked toward her on unsteady legs, watching her every move.

"I don't want you. How dare you, you . . ." she stopped as he lunged for her. He was slightly impaired with the amount of grog he had drunk. She easily side stepped him and jumped on the bed. Moving more carefully too the bed he smiled lazily at her. *By the gods and goddesses he was so handsome,* "You won't get away that easily." He slurred his words. Grabbing the end of the bed he steadied himself.

Anger and disgust showed on her beautiful face, "you are drunk!" she spoke accusingly.

"Yes, but not so drunk that I can't have my pleasure with you Lyssa." Walking around the bed slowly for if he walked to fast he thought his knees might go out from under him. Stopping right in front of her, breathing heavily, "You are so beautiful, your long blonde hair is like spun golden threads." Taking a deep breath, "Your scent is like honey and spices we grow in fields. Your skin is like the color of soft pink flowers."

His eyes blurred, "You know I love you Elena I have always loved you." Trying to focus he slowly walked toward her. "Your lips are red as the ruby gems on Zephron." He had reached out for her but swinging her body off the bed quickly she ran from him, her eyes filling with tears.

He was saying the words she had wanted to hear from him. She loved his blue/black hair that flowed to his shoulders, his dark blue colored eyes with the silver rims that sparkled when he looked at her. His lips were full and kissable, she liked the way his shoulders were strong and powerful. His wide chest made her skin blush. His enormous sex made her weak in the knees, she wanted him but she was so confused. She had missed his lips on hers and his hands as the cupped her breast and made her hunger for him.

When she had heard him speak Elena's name her anger flared. She was so caught up in her musings and anger that she didn't see him coming around the end of the bed. Grabbing her he kissed her deeply. She struggled with him at first pushing at his chest. "Stop Voltron, stop." She cried. "You don't want me leave me be, let go of me!" She raised her leg and hit him hard in the groin.

Voltron dropped her and fell to the ground. Pain clearly etched on his face. Getting up quickly Lyssa darted from the room, entering the cooking chamber she fell to the floor and sob her heart out.

Voltron passed out. The grog's effects finally placing him in blissful sleep. Lying on the floor in

Lyssa's room he began dreaming. He held Lyssa to him kissing her as she sighed into his mouth. Her hands moved to explore his wide chest. His tongue licked across her lips and she opened them to him. Plunging into her soft mouth he moaned, "Lyssa, you taste so sweet." She pushed him on his back and begun kissing and licking him from lips to his groin. The closer she got to his core the more he moaned, "Lyssa, please?"

Raising her head she looked into his eyes. "What do you want Voltron? Tell me."

"I need you. I want you. I love you." he declared. Love softened her eyes as she rose above him she lowering herself down on his throbbing shaft and road him till she felt her release. Breathless she leaned forward offering her breast to his lips. Taking one into his mouth he groaned as he felt her quickening the pace. Throwing his head back he grabbed her hips and rolled her over, lying between her legs he looked down and it wasn't Lyssa but Elena. She laughed as she disappeared from him taunting him. *"You are so mad if you think I ever loved you!" she said maliciously.* Suddenly it was Lyssa grabbing him crying out, "No, stop Voltron." *Why did she keep pushing at him, why did she want him to stop? What was wrong with her?*

Light panels started coming on in the room and woke Voltron. Coming awake he couldn't figure out why he was on the floor in Lyssa's room. Rising, he closed his eyes as the pain stabbed through his head. Rubbing his head he was trying to figure out what went on last night; looking around he wondered where Lyssa was? Rising slowly he went to his room to clean himself up and take some medication for his head. Walking out of his room he felt slightly better. Going in to the cooking chamber he found Lyssa on the floor.

He gently tried to awaken her. When she didn't respond he took her in his arms and walked her into her room where he laid her on the bed. Still not able to wake her he covered her with the bed covers and let her sleep.

As soon as Voltron left, Lyssa rolled over looking at the closed door. Tears running down her cheeks again, she was so tired of crying. She just couldn't get away from Elena. Feeling sick Lyssa rushed into the cleansing chamber and retched. Cleaning herself up, she lay back down. *Why am I so tired and sick? It's the stress it has to be. Maybe it was the lack of exercise. Maybe I could convince Voltron to let me train again.*

In the command center Voltron was puzzled at why Lyssa had been on the cooking chamber floor. He remembered she had been in her room when he went to find her last night. Rubbing his red rimmed eyes he swore to himself *why can't I remember?*

Betel took one look at Voltron seeing his red eyes and foul mood he wondered what had happened last night. Keeping his thoughts to himself he just shook his head and returned to his log report.

Sitting at the console Voltron tried to remember what had happened last night, he remembered drinking several glasses of grog. *No wonder my head is throbbing. I was mad at Tiernan for taking Lyssa's side. What happened after that he just couldn't remember?* Rubbing his face he rose, from his chair he carefully walked out of the command center. He needed the healer to give him something stronger for his throbbing head.

Entering sick bay Voltron spoke to Belgorod. "I need something for this ache in my head?"

Belgorod stood by the medical cart looking at Voltron. "You look like you wrestled with a *Cureralian* badger."

"Just give me something for my head?"

"Voltron maybe it's time to find out why she vexes you so." Taking two analgesics from a bottle then filling a cup with water he handed them to Voltron.

Downing the medication he leaned against the medical bed.

"You know Voltron," Belgorod said, "You cannot have it both ways with Lyssa. The Zephronians where genetically made to mate and love for life. Elena broke the chain when she left you. You are going to kill yourself if you don't decide soon whether you want Lyssa to stay and be your mate or let her leave." Sighing he placed his hand on Voltron's shoulder "If you love her then mate her for life. Keeping her as your sex toy is killing you." Letting go he turned back to the medical cart.

"I have mated with her I did the binding ritual however I do not love her. I can never love her because if I do then she will break my heart as well." He sighed

Hitting the com on his shoulder he called Betel, "I am going back to my quarters. Let me know if there are any other communications from Tiernan, Voltron out."

Taking the tram to his quarters he walked in quietly not wanting to wake Lyssa. Going back to her room he let himself in, sitting on the bed he caressed her face. *She looks so beautiful I ache just looking at her.* Rising quietly from the bed he looked down at her sleeping form. Walking to the door he was determined to try and love her after all she wasn't Elena.

Humming as he made his way to the cooking chamber he vowed to make a romantic dinner the first in a long line of plans to seduce Lyssa.

Lyssa woke up still feeling bad. Getting up she went into the cleansing chamber and bathed. Walking out into the hall she heard Voltron humming. Frowning she wondered what why he was humming. Shrugging her shoulders she moved further into the cooking chamber where her senses were assaulted by the delicious aromas. Curious she went to the stove and peeked into the pan.

Hearing her he turned and smiled at her. "I trust you are ok? You were sleeping still when I returned."

"I am fine to what do I owe this?" she waved her hand around the kitchen. He just smiled at her. She left to go to the table and lifting one of her pastries she started eating it. Gulping it down she was surprised at how hungry she was. Reaching for another one she looked up seeing Voltron watching her. Smiling sheepishly she said, "I am hungry."

Grunting he smiled at her, "Well don't ruin your appetite, I am making another dish from my home planet that I think you will enjoy."

Going to the oven chamber she saw that he was cooking what looked like some kind of avian. With a quizzical stare she looked up into his smiling face. "It is called sautéed phasianidae. I have also prepared mashed root vegetable and some of my own bread that I had Ea make me. My purple berry gooey cake, I think you will enjoy it. We have about five minutes and things will be done."

Leaving the phasianidae baking he went to the table, pouring the grog he then lit the candles. Going back into the cooking chamber he dished up their plates and returned placing them down, he pulled her chair out for her indicating that she should sit. Going back to the oven chamber he pulled the phasianidae out and took it to the table. Once there he carved it for her and gave her a generous piece.

Sitting "Well dig in." he said with a smile.

She was so hungry that she didn't need any more urging. Tasting everything first to make sure she would like it, she smiled at the taste of the phasianidae, eyes widening she smiled and looked at Voltron shaking her head as she took a big bite.

Licking the last of the phasianidae from her fingers she smiled up at Voltron. His breath caught in his throat. "Oh that was the most delicious thing I think I have ever eaten!" she exclaimed.

"Good I am glad that you liked it. Would you like some of our famous Zephronian dessert?" he grinned at her.

Nodding she said "Yes," excitedly licking her lips.

Rising he hoped his erection wasn't too evident as hurried to the kitchen to get the dessert. Placing it in front of her he dished up a large portion. She picked up a large piece and popped it in to her mouth.

Sitting he served himself a large piece. Lifting up his grog to her he saluted her, "*Quag* Lyssa." Lifting her glass she saluted him back, "*Quag* Voltron."

Taking a deep drink she smiled at him. Continuing she finished her dessert and sat back. "This was most excellent Voltron. I had no idea you could cook so well?"

"My mother insisted that her son's know how to cook just in case our mate's didn't know how."

He smiled but quickly stopped when he saw pain cross her face. "What's wrong Lyssa? Are you ill?"

Shaking her head no she fought but lost the battle to keep the tears from falling. "I am sick and tired of hearing about Elena, she left you but I am here." Crying out her pain, "You took me even though I was an innocent." Rising from her chair she yelled. "I took medication to stop from feeling aroused by you but it could not stop my heart from loving you. Yet you don't love me, I am nothing more than a toy for your sexual appetite Voltron." Putting her hand to her mouth she cried even more, "I don't understand, I can't understand how you would be so cruel. I, I . . ." turning she ran from the eating room.

Jumping up he ran after her. Barging into her room he went to her bed and knelt by it taking her gently in his arms. "Please don't cry Lyssa," he pleaded. Rolling her over so he could see her face, he gently wiped away the tears noticing she was very pale.

Suddenly feeling sick she pushed at his chest, "Let me go!" She tried getting up, he held on to her. "Voltron please I'm sick." Before he could let go of her she threw up all the food she had eaten. Voltron was shocked. Rising, he quickly carried her into the cleansing chamber where she continued to retch. Holding her head until she was done, he reached into the wall shelf getting a cloth to wash her face with. Still holding her as she began to tremble he was overcome with fear. Lifting her into his arms he turned and ran through the quarter and out into the corridor. Stopping the tram he rushed in as the tram whisked him back to the base.

He had been standing outside the sick bay door too long, getting angrier at the delay, finally he stormed in to where Lyssa lay sleeping on the bed as a med unit worked on her to restore the water she lost while getting sick. Her face was still so pale.

Going to her side he knelt down on one knee taking her hand in his. "I am so sorry," burying his head in her hand, "I didn't mean to make you ill." He cried. Feeling a hand on his shoulder he rose, quickly wiping the moisture out of his eyes.

"She will be fine Voltron. But there is something you should know. She is carrying your child." He said crossing his arms over his chest.

Voltron's knees buckled underneath him and he landed squarely on his bottom.

Belgorod quickly bent to help him up. "Are you ok Voltron?"

Still in a stupor Voltron slowly nodded his head.

"I am going to; I mean I was going to, Um." Stopping in midsentence he looked at the healer.

Finally the full impact of what Belgorod said hit him. Smiling up at the healer he grabbed his hand and shook it. "I was in the process of wooing her when she got sick. I thought I had somehow poisoned her with my cooking," Smiling from ear to ear he asked, "Are you sure Belgorod?"

"Yes I am sure, very sure."

"When can I take her back to my quarters?" he asked softly.

"As soon as she wakes you can take her home with you. I will be giving her some medication for the nausea and that should help." Turning he left the two alone in sick bay.

Sitting by her bed he reached out and picked up her hand placing it next to his heart. "How can you ever forgive me for being so cruel to you?"

She tightened her gripe on his hand and he looked up. "I loved you the first time you took me. I have never loved another you are the only one for me Voltron." She spoke softly. Voltron smiled at her as he placed his head on the bed. *She loves me, even as cruel and mean as I have been to her she loves me.* Voltron's heart was beginning to break only this time it was breaking with the first rays of loves he hadn't felt in a long time. How had this little slip of a female gotten into his heart?

Calum, Boden and Vaughn sat outside in the court yard bar. They were waiting for an informant so they could send a message to the Galactic Council.

"He should have been here by now." Fumed Boden.

"He will be, take it easy." Calum said.

"Who on the council is our ally?" Vaughn asked.

"He has asked me to keep his name quite." He must be wealthy though by the number of dinaries he gave for information regarding the Zephron gems."

"Good, when this job is done we should be able to leave this part of the galaxy and never be heard from again." Boden smiled clapping Vaughn on the shoulder.

A wizened sickly green creature sat beside the three men. "Is it I you wait for?" he asked in a guttural voice.

Jumping when they heard him he laughed in as he moved to their table. "Mes a thinkin you are not here for me?" he glared at them

"We are if you are from the council?" Calum spoke.

"Mes is him. Does you have messaged to give me?" he reached his greasy grimy covered three fingered paw to them.

Calum reached into his pocket and pulled out a vid-pad. Starting to give it to the ugly creature he pulled back. "Do you have our dinaries?"

Sneering, the ugly creature took the sack of dinaries from his pouch and threw it at them. "Heres a bees you dinaries. Give you me give you me." He reached once again taking the vid-pod.

"How soon can we expect to hear from you again?" Calum asked. *If he had his way he would rather not met with this revolting creature again.*

"Mes a not know, mes a thinkin yousa very dumb man." Pulling out his gun the ugly creature shot Calum in the chest before Calum even knew what was happening. Leaping up he sprang thirty feet into the air and got away before Vaughn and Boden had a chance to get out of their chairs.

"Calum!" Vaughn yelled reaching down he placed his fingers on Calum's neck there was no heartbeat. Vaughn's eyes were filled with terror, *why had they killed Calum?* Boden was pulling on Vaughn yelling, "Get up get up the constabulary is on their way." Pulling hard on Vaughn Boden helped him up. Turning, they both ran just as the authorities arrived at the outside bar.

The ugly little creature brought the vid-pod to Killian. "Mes a got u for."

Reaching down Killian took the vid-pod from Grenif. Watching the vid cast he smiled evilly. "Yousa seems happy mesa a thinkin." Smiled Grenif.

"Yes this is better than what we first thought. Those gems we stole from Zephron are very powerful. They will suit our needs well." Laughing he threw a ripe polmab fruit to Grenif who quickly grabbed it biting into the succulent fruit smiling at his master.

Walking out of his study Killian smiled at himself, *I won't need Tess that disgusting bitch. Now I will rule as many planets as I can conquer with Zephron's gems.*

Fleeing in the skimmer, Boden and Vaughn were stunned. Their friend and companion had been killed and for what? "Vaughn there has to be more to those gems than even Calum knew about." Concentrating on the flight coordinates, "yes, why would they kill Calum, they came to us to steal the gems we didn't seek them out." Vaughn spoke quietly still trying to understand what had happened.

Boden went back to the steering console and begin to hatch a plan. He wanted more that his fair share of the money given for the stolen gems. He wanted the gems himself. What had been on the vid pod that made the ugly little creature kill Calum? Slamming his fist down he swore to himself, *I don't know but I will find out.*

It had been several minutes later that Vaughn approached Boden, "The plan as Calum made said we need to take Lyssa and return her to King Zarift. He felt we would get more money that way. Do you agree?"

Turning in his chair he looked at Vaughn sighing he shrugged his shoulders, "we have nothing to do but to follow Calum's plan right?" He asked, "I think we should try and contact Princess Tess and tell her that Calum's dead. I know Calum didn't like Tess but with her plan we were going to be rich beyond compare. I think we should follow through and kidnap Lyssa and go from there."

Vaughn nodded, "You are right if we veer off the path now they will find us out for sure. I don't want that. When do we report back to Commander Tiernan?"

"We have twenty one more days before we report for duty again. Pray the gods and goddesses that we will be done with this and on our way out of this galaxy."

CHAPTER FOUR

True Enemy Revealed

Stretching Lyssa realized Voltron was no longer in bed with her. Saddened at the loss of his warmth she rose wrapping the sheet around her going to her room to dress. She was hungry.

When she reached the cooking chamber she was disappointed in not seeing Voltron there. Lifting the lid to the fruit breads she grabbed one to eat smiling as she did. Voltron had not realized what they were when she first made them. Tasting one he had gotten the most amazing smile on his face as he devoured the entire tray. Taking two bites Lyssa decided that she would wrap up some and take them to Voltron on the base. Walking back to her room she went to the cleansing chamber and showered. Looking down her swelling belly she was surprised at how big she had gotten. *Well it's a loose tunic for me* she smiled to herself.

Entering the tram Lyssa smiled hoping the gift of these treats would show him how much she cared and how her heart had warmed at his confession of love for her. The Sentry at the gate bowed his head to her as she passed through. It took her no time at all to reach the building that housed the communication center. Stepping up to the door it swished open so she could go through the portal. She waited a few seconds so her eyes could adjust to the semi dark interior. Looking around she saw Voltron and started for him when the building exploded in front of her. Screaming out his name she ran to where she thought he was, not finding him she began to search, suddenly she felt arms come around her waist. Relaxing she thought it was Voltron. Turning in his arms she realized immediately that it wasn't and she started to scream. Back handing her hard she fell limp in his arms. Boden grabbed her. Princess Tess would be pleased. Not only had he killed Voltron, but he had managed to grab Lyssa. Carrying her back to the star skimmer he threw Lyssa down on a bunk before barking orders to Vaughn to lift off before the star base recovered.

Voltron fought the darkness that threatened to take him. Betel inched forward on his hands and knees calling out to his Prince. "Commander, where are you?"

Clearing his throat Voltron tried to speak. All he was able to get out was a grunt as the darkness over took him. Reaching Voltron, Betel bent over him and lifted him. Taking him to the door where they both collapsed. Arielle, Oden and Arthur had been standing just outside the door when the blast occurred. They raced into the command center helping the injured crew. Arielle brought Voltron and Betel to sick bay. Belgorod stood over them with medical unit scanning their bodies. Breathing a sigh of relief he spoke to Arielle, "Your brother and Betel are fine, just a little shaken."

"You are sure there is no damage to them?" Arielle asked concern for both men.

"Yes I am sure." He replied.

"I will return to the command center and tell the crew that they will recover." With that Arielle left

The command center was a cacophony of activity as the crew worked vigorously to clean up the mess the blast had made. Walking in from sick bay Voltron spoke to the men, "How did they get past our outer defenses?"

"No one is sure. One minute there was no one there and the next we were reeling from the energy blast." Brice spoke

"Put a call into Tiernan! Now" Voltron ordered.

"Voltron, I sent a communications to Tiernan he is on his way here. He should be arriving in less than thirty minutes. We were lucky he was just docking with the space station when I messaged him." Arielle spoke concern in his voice for his older brother.

"When he comes, Arielle, bring him and Betel into my private office."

Pacing Voltron waited for Tiernan and Betel to arrive. He was so furious with himself. I should have been ready for another attack from the Zariftians. Now his command center lay in ruins and it would take days to fix all the monitors, communication boards and Intel system that the energy blast had taken out.

Sitting at his desk he placed his head in his hands. The blast had given him a bad head ache. Where were the two why was it taking so long?

Rushing into the command center Tiernan turned as Betel called his name.

"This way Commander Tiernan."

Following Betel to Voltron's private office, "Voltron, what happened?"

"We were attacked on our own star base."

"What, that's impossible! We have an excellent defense system. How could they get past it?" Tiernan asked.

"I'm not sure Tiernan, but I would say we have a traitor in our midst." Betel agreed that someone on the inside would have to know how to disarm the security system to get that close to our moon base command center.

"If that is true Voltron, then we can't be too careful in our communications between each other. I will send Arielle a new communication device encoded so that we can talk to each other without others listening in on our conversations. I am heading back to the surface of Zephron will you accompany me? I will be sending the galactic council a communication telling them we have been attacked on our moon base. I will be leaving for Zephrite in thirty minutes" with that he left.

The men had done a good job at cleaning up the command center. Look around he knew though it would take days to fix the electronics. Voltron was tired he spoke to Maddox the Engineer officer, "I'm going to my quarters." Maddox's nodded and turned his attention back to the damaged control panel.

Walking toward the base gate the security guard Rilen stopped Voltron. "Is Miss Lyssa alright sir?" he asked concern etched on his face.

Looking confused he shook his head, "Yes, she is fine."

Relief flooded Rilen's face. "Oh thank the gods and goddesses. I was so worried when she arrived at the same time the command center blew up."

"What the hell are you talking about Rilen? Lyssa was never in the command center!" he spoke harshly to the young sentry guard.

"But sir, I mean Prince Voltron . . ." he swallowed, "I had just admitted Miss Lyssa into the gate right before the blast. She had a plate of food for you." he said afraid.

Fear struck Voltron, then rage. Whoever attacked the base now had her. Turning quickly he went back to find Betel and Arielle. "They dared to attack our moon base and they took Lyssa. Rilen said he had let her in to bring me food. She has never done that before." Anger filled his face.

Waking up in the bunk on a star skimmer, Lyssa struggled to regain consciousness. Where was she and why did her cheek hurt. Rising slowly, she looked around. *This looks like one of our star skimmers. How did I get here?* Hearing the captain of the star skimmer murmuring into a communication device she stood up, nausea hit her hard and she sat back down. Hearing the noise behind him Boden turned to see that Lyssa was awake.

Rising he went to her glaring at her. "Well it's about time you came around!" he said as he meanly rubbed the bruise on her cheek.

"Why am I here?" she asked trying to take steading breaths so she would not retch.

"That's for me to know and you to find out." Reaching out he just had to touch her hair. When she slapped at his hand he roughly grabbed her breast and twisted it. She screamed out in pain. This only seemed to egg him on. Bending down he grabbed her hair yanking her head up bringing her mouth close to his. "Oh little Lyssa, I am so going to enjoy teaching you the way to please a man." He snarled.

Laughing she glanced around the skimmer "Well I don't see any men here so who would teach me these lessons?" She mocked him. Pulling her up by her hair Boden grabbed her dress and began ripping it. As she screamed Boden back handed her again. *Sometimes my mouth is my worst enemy.*

Vaughn jumped from the navigator's chair. "Stop it Boden, she is a Princess of Zarift and even though I am sure Tess would like us to hurt her, I am sure her father will pay well for her return. Remember what Calum said regarding her."

"Yes I remember but he is dead. It is just you and I now." Boden snarled.

Lyssa's head came up with a jolt at hearing her sister's name. What on earth did Tess have to do with this before she could ask Vaughn what he meant but Boden hit her again, knocking her unconscious?

Privately Boden sent a message to Princess Tess,

Calum is dead. I have Lyssa. Vaughn doesn't want to kill her. I am going to kill both by leaving them stranded on the planet Kian. We have hidden the gems in a safe place, when King Zephron, Voltron and the other princes' are dead I will bring them to you. Until then I will be hiding out. Boden

Tiernan joined Voltron, Arielle and Arlana they were to returning to their father's palace in Zephite City.

Entering the palace the Kings children stood before him. Voltron was barely able to contain his rage and anger at Lyssa being taken. "Father who ever attacked our moon base also took Lyssa, my mate. She is carries my child."

Queen Aiofe looked up from her sewing when she heard Princess Lyssa's name, "What do you mean was Princess Lyssa on our moon base?"

"Yes I took her when she attacked me. I have mated with her mother and she carries my child." He spoke.

Queen Aiofe sat back down dumbfounded by her son's response. "She carries your child the next Zephron heir?" cried Aiofe.

"Yes, are you unhappy with this mother? I would have thought you would have been ecstatic since you all wanted me mated!" He stormed. For the first time Aiofe looked into Voltron's eyes and saw a life there, even though his voice did not convey his love for Lyssa his eye sure did and she had not seen that look for several months. Looking directly at Voltron Aiofe spoke, "You are in love with her?"

"I am mother."

Arielle interrupted, "Father, I have a communication from the Galactic Council. It was just sent to me from the Erne."

King Zephron looked at Arielle, "Plug it into out communication screen so we all can hear what they are saying."

Be it known that the unwarranted attack on Zephron's Royal City Zephrite and their outpost on Varian. We the Galactic Council find the Zarifts negligence in waging war against the Zephrons. King Zarift is to make restitution for any and all damaged incurred by the Zephronians. If King Zarift continues in war he will be stripped of his royal rank and another shall be put in his place as ruling King. This decree is set forth this star date 2022.33.001.

"The decree has been signed by all the royal heads of the Galactic Council." Arielle said.

"We have until the Athnam to find out what started all this? I am at a loss as to why this took place since the mating ritual and binding was signed by both ruling families. Did they have no intention of honoring it from the start?" fumed King Zephron.

"I don't know nor care now father, the only thing I am worried about is Lyssa and the child. We have to find her soon. If they have hurt her I will kill them."

"As soon as the video log of the command center is repaired we will know who took Lyssa." Tiernan said.

"How soon will you have that footage?"

"I will personally see to it myself father." Arielle rose to leave as he spoke.

"Make it happen quickly son."

"Son you look exhausted why not go and lie down until the video is repaired." Aiofe said.

Going to his room to rest he decided to pour himself a drink. Running his hand through his hair he sat there worrying about Lyssa. *What would he do if he didn't find her? If they hurt her he would kill them. By the gods and goddesses I will rip them apart.* He didn't hear his mother knock as she come into his room.

"Mother" he said rising as she walked to the couch.

She looked intently at Voltron, "Sit you are tired. There is another matter I need to discuss with you. One hundred and twenty days ago someone sent me a private vid. As I listen to the message it was about Elena and Cart." she sniffed. She noted that he had stiffened at hearing Elena's name.

Sitting back against the couch he sighed heavily, "Go on mother."

"My son, they found the bodies of Elena and Cart tortured and buried on the moon of Pleightese." Aiofe sniffled into her hand.

"What?" Stunned Voltron sat up quickly, "How? Pleightese?" he asked, "it didn't make sense why would they go there and not leave the galaxy entirely?"

"I don't understand myself. The tip on the vid-pod showed our warriors where to find the graves. However, we don't know who the tip was from. The vid-pod could not be traced" She placed her arm around Voltron. "My son I am so sorry."

"You say they had been tortured?" he asked scowling.

"Yes, your father's warriors investigated it along with your brother Tiernan. We ask Tiernan not to tell you just yet. We have not told anyone else about Elena's death. We were afraid that someone might come after you."

"So you think they were killed because Elena had been my mate and had information on how to use our gems?" he asked slumping back into the couch as confusion, anger and sadness moved across his face.

"We thought she might have been tortured so she would give them the technology of the gems. It saddens me as Elena never knew of the power or the technology of the gems. She died for nothing." Placing a kiss on her son's forehead she rose to leave.

"Mother?"

"Yes," she turned back to Voltron

"Thank you."

She turned quickly so Voltron would not see the tears that threatened to fall down her cheeks.

Rising Voltron strode to his bed. Stripping he fell naked on to the bed. Burying his face in his pillow he cried out his sorrow at losing Elena, he just couldn't lose Lyssa and his child as well.

King Zephron sat at his desk signing papers there was a knock on the door interrupting his work. "Yes, come in."

"Your Majesty I have a vid-pod communication for you." Jasper said as he handed the king the vid-pad. Turning to leave Jasper stopped, "Is there anything else you wish Sire?"

"Yes Jasper, will you have Voltron and the others come to my office?"

Jasper nodded to the king as he turned to leave going to get Prince Voltron and the others.

Turning his attention to the vid-pod he was surprised to see it was from King Zarift.

We have Princess Lyssa if Voltron wants her back he needs to meet us at the Athnam. We will bring her there, be sure to bring a Zephron gem for her ransom. You can thank Vaughn and Boden for her capture.

The voice laughed evilly before ending the pod-cast, Voltron thought he knew the voice but couldn't place it.

King Zephron laid the vid-pad down. He had not realized that Voltron had entered the room and heard what the unknown person was saying.

"Father you asked me to come to your office."

"Did you hear what the ransom is for Lyssa?" he asked.

"I did." Voltron snarled.

"I commed Arielle and he has the video of the blast on Varian. He should be here soon. Please sit. Tiernan is also on his way here."

Nodding he sat, "I don't understand, how did Vaughn and Boden could get their hands on Lyssa? They weren't even on Varian when we were attacked. They were on Tiernan's star ship." Voltron stated.

"I have had Tiernan and his crew investigating the deaths of Elena and Cart. I think that if we are to find any answers it will be in continuing the investigation of their deaths."

"Father," said Arielle and bowed his head, "I have the video." Coming toward his father and Voltron, he laid the vid-pad on his father's desk. Tiernan walked in just as Arielle pressed the button turning on the video. They all watched as the command center's crew went about their routine activities. Five minutes into the video an energy blast went off, they watched as Voltron crumpled to the floor, and then they heard Lyssa cry out his name. From behind her someone grabbed her. They couldn't make out the face yet, but as he turned to leave he back handed Lyssa and she passed out. His face was then clearly visible it was Boden. Hitting the stop button the room remained silent.

Anger seize Voltron as he roared, "I will kill him for touching my mate." Spinning around he ran toward the doors with Arielle in hot pursuit. Going to the transportation bay Voltron hit the com button on his lapel, speaking to the crew of the Erne, "transport."

Arriving in the transporter room Voltron went directly to the bridge. "Are you ready to leave the docking bay?" he asked Orin.

"Yes Commander, we have just finished off loading ships supplies and are ready for your coordinates."

"Crew of the Erne, we will be traveling to Pleightese, my brother's ship the Talisman will be following us there as well. We hope to find out information as to the where Boden and Vaughn are and who killed Elena and Cart." Orin take us out of the docking bay."

As Orin press buttons and levers, the ship slid from its docking port, "Commander we are clear of the docking bay."

"Orin go to hyper drive on my mark, 3, 2, 1"

Hitting the engines hyper drive the Erne leapt forward in to the black and starry universe.

Turning to Orin, "How long before we arrive on Pleight?" Voltron asked.

"We should arrive in seven days," Replied Orin. "I will be in my office."

The star skimmer landed on the planet Kian. Getting up from the console Boden went to see if Lyssa was still sleeping. He turning quietly and quickly taking his stun gun and he brought down hard on Vaughn's head knocking him out. *I will not give Lyssa back and be tried for kidnapping, I will take Princess Tess the news she has wanted to hear; Voltron is dead and so is her little sister.*

Lifting Lyssa from the bunk Boden took her down to the planet's surface depositing her on the soil. Returning to the skimmer he brought Vaughn's body and took him to the surface laying him beside Lyssa. Returning a final time to the skimmer Boden started the ships engines and lifted off the planet.

Voltron had sent a communications to Tiernan on the secure vid-pad. "Tiernan, where are your warriors Vaughn and Boden?"

"They are on leave they have been for twenty one days." replied Tiernan."

"It was Boden he kidnapped her."

"By the stars of Zephron, my own crew," he stormed "They are due back today I will make sure my Warriors place them in the holding cell for questioning."

Trying to open her eyes Lyssa squinted at the soft pink light. Her head was throbbing. Sitting up she fought the nausea that threatened to spill out. Looking around slowly she tried to remember how she got here. Hearing a moan at her back she turned quickly and saw a form of a man lying on the ground. Tuning she rose on her knees and turned him over she saw it was Vaughn. Everything came rushing back to her. Gently shaking Vaughn he finally opened his eyes.

"Warrior Vaughn, are you ok?" she asked

Placing a hand to the back of his head he found a big nodule. Shaking his head yes he was rewarded with an agonizing stab of pain. Struggling to rise he held his hand out to Lyssa as she helped him sit up. "Where are we?" he asked.

"I don't know. The last thing I remember is Boden hitting me while on the ship."

Looking at this small princesses facing him, Vaughn was angry and disgusted with Boden. Lifting his hand he touched the large bruise on the left side of her face. "I am sorry Princes, I had no idea that Boden would do this to you or me for that matter." Hanging his head in shame he continued, "Stealing the gems from Zephron is what we were paid to do."

"You, you stole the gems? It wasn't even Zariftian warriors?" she was furious as she stood. "All this could have been avoided."

"Your sister and Duke Killian paid Calum, Boden and I to steal the gems."

"My sister?" she stomped her foot in her anger, "I knew Tess hated our father but I didn't think she would stoop to this."

"Well you won't like what I have to tell you about her then," he paused and looked at her.

"Well go on!" she stormed.

"Princess Tess sought us out, she wanted us to kill Voltron, his father and you." again he hung his head in shame.

"What, why that mean spirited vial *Carmen*," she sputtered and fumed, "Wait till I get my hands on her. She will rue the day she was birthed."

Smiling at her spirit he spoke and pointed to the sky, "Be that as it may my princess we need to find shelter. It looks like a storm is coming."

Turning toward where Vaughn was pointed she saw the angry looking red, black and gray clouds in the sky. She helped Vaughn to his feet and together they sought shelter before the storm hit. As they walked Lyssa asked, "Do you know what planet we are on?"

"Yes it is the planet Kian."

Concerned she asked, "What isn't that where all the severe atmospheric storms are?"

"Yes that is why we must hurry princess." Walking a little faster they arrived at the outcropping of rocks just as the severe wind and rain hit. Huddling in the shelter of the outcropping Vaughn laid back to rest. Sitting beside him Lyssa lay back as well. She wondered what Voltron was doing? Did he miss her as much as she missed him? At the thought of his father the baby leapt in her womb. Smiling she placed a loving hand over her swelling belly. *Soon my little love your daddy will come and find us.*

Vaughn noticed her hands placed lovingly over her swollen belly. "By the gods and goddesses I had no idea you were with child?"

"No one but Voltron, and Healer Belgorod know. We haven't told anyone yet."

Voltron and Security Warrior Brice had transported to the surface of Pleight. Meeting up with his brother Voltron asked about the investigation, "Have you found any other clues?"

"No not really, we have been over this surface a thousand times and still no clues as to who did this, just the usual things, broken vegetation, rocks that covered the bodies. There are no clear foot prints. Even the absence of blood is baffling. If they were tortured and killed here there should have at least been some blood." Tiernan said.

Kneeling Voltron looked at the makeshift graves that had housed Elena and Cart. Looking at the ground where his first love laid in death hurt his heart more than he wanted to admit. Rising he spoke to Tiernan, "That tells me then that they were killed somewhere else and brought here to throw us off as to who really did this."

"Yes that is my conclusion as well" Tiernan said as he dusted the dirt off his hands. Looking around he shielded his eyes, "Don't you think we would have at least found a boot print. There are no wind or air disturbances on this planet. A boot imprint would have remained in the soil it would still be here. However, if you look here someone wiped them out. Notice these striations across here that lead to where a skimmer had landed." Tiernan pointed out.

"Yes I see." Voltron walked to where the skimmer had landed. Squatting he looked at the imprint the skimmer had made in the soil. "You know the feet of the skimmer have unusual markings, see the three horizontal lines next to the two vertical lines I have seen those markings somewhere else I just can't remember where." Rising he turned to his brother, have Boden and Vaughn check in yet."

"No, I have placed several communications to them and they have not responded. Calum my Chief Science Officers is missing as well"

"I don't know what to make of this." Voltron said. "It looks more and more like Boden and Vaughn were involved in stealing the gems." Pausing he looked in Tiernan's eyes, "Do you think they murdered Elena and Cart?"

"I believe if we find out who stole the gems we might find out who killed Elena and Cart. My gut tells me they are involved but I just can't be sure."

Placing his hand on Voltron shoulder Tiernan spoke, "Let's get back to the ship and have Betel run tests on these soil samples and see if anything turns up."

Seated at the lab desk, Betel was busy looking at the samples they had brought on board. "These dirt samples give no vital information." Betel spoke to Voltron still looking through the spectrometer.

Sitting at the table in the Betel's lab Voltron was clearly worried. "I am worried about Lyssa!"

Turning from his work Betel he looked at Voltron, "She will be alright she is very spirited. She took you out didn't she," he smiled at Voltron, "so I think she will be able to take care of herself."

"Not this time Betel she carries my child!"

"What?" was all that Betel got out he was so shocked at what Voltron had said.

"She carries my child." Rubbing his hand through his long hair he shook his head. "I will admit that I had never wanted another mate. Elena had so broken my heart that I just didn't want the pain again." Rising he went to the view screen and watched as the stars speed by in the velvety blackness. "She is so small and yes she is spirited. But could she protect herself and the babe? What if they kill her and my child?" his voice choked. Clearing his throat he said, "I will kill Boden for touching her as he did, she is my mate and no man shall touch her as I saw him touch her."

Betel had been quiet up to this point, "Voltron my old friend my heart burst with a joy that you have found a mate again. At the same time it is burden with your worry. We will find her and we will punish Boden and Vaughn for their part in this. Until then let's concentrate on where they might be."

It had been seven days that Vaughn and Lyssa were on Kian. Lyssa arose from the hard ground her back killing her. Looking down she could have sworn that her belly had gotten bigger overnight. Seeing that Vaughn still slept she decided to find a secluded place to relieve herself. Following the cliff for a few feet she saw that the vegetation was thick enough to be private.

Waking Vaughn stretched. He was going to kill Boden when found him. Startled out of his revere by a scream Vaughn was suddenly aware that Princess Lyssa was not by his side. Jumping up he listened trying to find out where the scream came from, there it was again, running in the direction of the scream he hoped and prayed nothing bad had happened to her,

Picking up a large branch of a purple tree Lyssa swung at the beast again. "Oh no you don't mister sneaking up on me and making my heart jump out of my chest." She swung again at the large beast. He just watched her as she swung the thing at him, inhaling deeply the beast tried to sniff her again. She hit him on the head with the large branch. Yowling in pain the large beast took a stand and charged Lyssa. Jumping to one side Lyssa brought the branch down hard on the beasts back causing it to yowl again. Just as the beast was going to charge again Lyssa tripped over a branch buried in the soil. Lying on her back side she tried to roll but her belly wasn't letting move very quickly. The beast jumped almost pouncing on her when he fell to the ground dead.

"Are you alright Princess?" Vaughn asked concern written on his face. Rushing to her side he helped her stand. Looking at her swollen belly he asked "Where you that big yesterday?" Vaughn looked at Lyssa belly worried etched in his face.

Pulling her hands free from him she fumed, "No, it seems that Voltron's baby wants to be as big as his father." Turning she stormed off with Vaughn yelling at her to wait for him.

"Princess I didn't mean that. It just concerns me that your belly is twice as big as it was yesterday. Are you feeling ok?" he asked as he caught up with her which wasn't too hard to do as she was waddling along the side of the cliff making her way back to the outcropping.

"Oh, I am not mad at you Vaughn, it was that dumb beast that scared me and then I could not fight it off very well. The baby was in the way." She shrugged "I am not use to not being able to defend myself." Reaching the outcropping Lyssa sat down weary from her little run in with the beast.

Vaughn squatted down, "I will go and see what the vegetation has to offer in the way of nourishment, I will go and get some water to drink. Will you be alright here while I am gone?" he asked hesitant to leave her.

"I'll be fine, just leave me your gun. That should . . . she yawn . . . . be fine." Laying her head down on the ground she curled around her baby and went to sleep again.

"Voltron, I have intercepted a message from Princess Tess to Boden." Arielle said.

Grabbing the vid-pad he read the message, "Warrior Boden I received your message stating you abducted my bitch of a sister. With Voltron dead and you leaving her and Vaughn on Kian, our mission will be a success. My father has no idea that I bought you, Vaughn or Calum to help me steal the gems from Zephron. It saddens me that your torture of Elena and Cart did not get the technology we need to make the gems into a weapon, but you have delivered on the other items. Duke Killian and I will make sure you have a place in the new kingdom once my father is dead. Stay hidden until the Athnam on Barax. Keep communications to a minimum. You will hear from me soon until then stay hidden. Tess.

"By the gods of Zephron the witch has planned this from the beginning." Slamming down the vid-pad he stormed off the bridge. "Deck 4" he stormed.

Entering his private quarters Voltron went to the food panel and punched the order for a grog, sitting at the table he sipped it slowly to let his anger ease. Getting up he tapped the com on his shirt, "Chief Science officer Betel, Ship's navigator Orin, weapons engineer Arthur, communications officer Arielle, security officer Brice, meet me in my ready room immediately, Voltron out." Leaving his quarters he returned to the ships bridge as he entered his ready room, the men were standing waiting for him.

"Arielle intercepted a communications from Princess Tess of Zarift. Listen as I play what she had to say."

Slamming their hands down on the table each of them bellowed their outrage.

"Betel you will take command of the ship, Orin you will plot a course to Varian, Arthur you and Brice will come with me to the skimmer. We will be leaving shortly Brice inform Belgorod to accompany us. Arielle get on the encrypted communications and send Tiernan a message to meet us on Varian's star base then send father a message as well. Tell him we have located Vaughn and Lyssa on Kian. Are we all in agreement?" Voltron asked.

"Aye Commander." They all said in unison.

CHAPTER FIVE

The Galactic Council's Athnam

$\mathcal{V}$aughn had not gone far when he found a small purple pond teaming with fish. Silently he neared the edge of the pond lying down on his stomach he reached in and caught a fish, then another and another. Once back with Lyssa he made a small fire and cooked the fish.

The smell was good as she inhaled. Opening her eyes she saw Vaughn cooking something on a small fire. Rising she went over and smiled at him. Trying to sit she had a sharp pain go through her. Vaughn jumped up and helped her down. Concern in his eye he asked, "Are you ok?"

"Yes, this baby is big and doesn't like me moving very much." Smiling she got as comfortable as she could.

"Are you hungry?"

"Yes famished." Talking a piece of the fish he offered it to her, "how long do you think it will take Voltron to find us?"

"It depends, if Orin can find a trace of the skimmer that we took then it shouldn't take too long to find where he left us." Lyssa moved uncomfortably and sought out a rock to lie back against. "It shouldn't be too long princess. Here have some water and if you like I can help you down to the pond later and you can cleanse yourself, would you like that?" he said smiling at her.

"That would be nice. But I think I will lay here for a little while longer. I am so tired." He watched her as her eyes closed again. He was quite concerned as to why she was so sleepy and tired all the time. Women of Zephron had no trouble carrying babies like what she was having. Sitting beside her he wondered at the rate of growth of the baby as well. She could only be at the most a month along or more into the pregnancy. If so the babe was growing fast almost too fast for her small body to keep up with it. Grinding his teeth he cursed

Boden the fool he could well have sealed Lyssa's death sentence by marooning us here. Where are you Voltron, please hurry otherwise you may put me to death for Lyssa and your child's death.

*　　*　　*　　*

"How much longer before we are there?" Voltron asked for the one hundredth time, pacing the floor on the bridge.

"We are there our ship is in range to transport you down to the surface if you will go to the transport bay commander." Orin spoke, "I have ordered Healer Belgorod to the transporter as well."

Running toward the elevator he yelled, "Transportation bay."

The weather on Kian was getting bad again. Vaughn woke Lyssa, there's another storm on the way princess, trying to rise she stumbled lifting her he carried her to the outcropping where they would weather the storm.

Landing on the planets surface, Voltron, Belgorod and Arthur grabbed their weapons and put them on stun. The wind was howling and the rain was coming down fierce. "Voltron we need to find cover," yelled Arthur. Scanning the horizon they all saw the high cliffs at the same time and headed in that direction.

Covering her body with his Vaughn tried keeping Lyssa dry. Curled around her baby she smiled up at him. "Thank you Vaughn, I will see that things don't go so hard on you. You have been so kind to me and my baby."

Smiling, "Princess if the truth be known I never really wanted any part in this scheme," hanging his head in shame, "there was no honor in what I did and I deserve whatever Prince Voltron and Prince Tiernan give me."

Suddenly Lyssa let out a strangled scream, the pain in her stomach so severe she thought she would be torn asunder. Reaching for Vaughn she grabbed his arm and squeezed it tight. Vaughn paled at the sound.

Running toward the cliffs Voltron was hit with a terrible pain in his stomach causing him to stumble and lose his footing. Arthur stopped and helped him up. "Are you alright commander?"

"Something must be wrong with Lyssa." He continued to run toward the cliffs in time to see Vaughn picking up Lyssa and moving her back farther into the cliff.

Running forward he grabbed her from Vaughn's arms. She screamed as he did so. Voltron paled, hitting the com he yelled five to transport NOW," he yelled. Leaving the skimmer on Kian they would return later for it.

As Voltron was getting them transported Belgorod commed MAILS have medics in the transportation bay at once.

Once in the bay Voltron gently laid Lyssa down on the medical cart. Noting her huge belly, he looked at Belgorod, "how can the baby be that big she is only a few months along." They walked quickly to sick bay Vaughn temporarily forgotten. Arthur took him to the holding cell. As Arthur turned to leave Vaughn spoke to him, "Please tell me if all is ok with Princess Lyssa." Arthur heard the pain in his voice and knew no punishment now would be worse than the punishment Vaughn was placing on himself. "I will get you updates." Then he left.

Sick bay was a mad house medical units spurting and sputtering, MAILS running diagnostic's on Lyssa quite form. Voltron huddled as close to her as he could without being in the healer's way so he could keep tabs on her and his child.

Nurse Gennie spoke to the healer, "Healer Belgorod, I have run a scan and have found out that the reason she is so large, in her womb she carries three life signs." Belgorod raised his eyebrows.

"I have scanned her twice and her life signs are good she is very small to be carrying three babies." For a moment Belgorod forgot about Voltron in the corner, turning to see him now he saw a white faced warrior who was in shock. Going to him he helped him down on to a chair.

"Three, there are three babies?" he questioned mystified. Patting Voltron on the shoulder Belgorod smiled at him, "Yes three my prince. You are having three," he paused. "MAILS have you determined the gender of the babies?"

"Yes Healer Belgorod there are two males and one female. All babies are doing fine." Clapping Voltron's shoulder again he said, "See, two healthy sons and one healthy daughter."

Arielle was waiting out in the corridor until he heard the medical unit say that she was carrying three babies rushing in smiling at his brother. "Job well done my brother, shall I send a message to mother and father to let them know they are going to be grandparents?" he anxiously looked at Voltron.

Jumping up and smiling he seemed to walk taller than his six feet six inch height. "Yes brother message the entire family included Lyssa's family. Let them know she is in good health. I am relinquishing command of my ship to Betel until I can make sure Lyssa and the babies are safe." The whole ship had been holding its breath it seemed like and when the word came down that Princess Lyssa and the babies where alright the whole crew let a war cry thanking the gods and goddesses that all was well.

"Voltron, I will keep her in sick bay for two days just to monitor her and the babies. When you take her back to your quarters she will not be able to move around too much on her own. She is so small and with three babies she is rather large and will have difficulty moving. You will have to see to her needs and carry her so she does not injury herself or the babies."

Nodding Voltron just lay his head on the side of the medical bed holding Lyssa's hand. *How I fought loving you yet even in your anger you loved me back and now you are carrying three of my babies inside your small body.* She squeezed his hand, lifting his head he saw that she looked at him with love and thanks. "I knew you would find us." She spoke softly. Lifting her hand she moved a lock of his beautiful blue/black hair from his forehead. "They will have your hair, my eyes but your strength." Rising Voltron leaned over and kissed her on the forehead. "I am so sorry that I was mean and indifferent to you. My heart and my soul now lie in your hands. I am hopelessly and utterly mated and in love with you Lyssa. There are no more ghosts between us. Elena's is gone from my heart forever." She pulled him in closed and kissing him deeply. "I love you my Prince my warrior of Zephron. I will always love you." The babies jumped in side her and she smiled, taking one of his hands and placing it on the movement. His eyes widened as he felt his unborn children move inside his mate. Lowering his mouth to her rounded stomach he spoke, "I love you and your mother more than life itself." He kissed her abdomen. Lyssa closed her eyes and sighed now that she was safe and loved all would be ok.

Two days later Voltron was able to bring Lyssa to his quarters. He never left her side. Everyday Betel would update him on their trip to the Athnam. There still was no word on Boden or Princess Tess. Every day as well Voltron's mother Aiofe came to visit with Lyssa. Voltron would not let anyone stay too long to tire her, not even his father or mother. They were meeting Tiernan and Arlana at the Athnam along with King Zarift and Queen Zephorah. One person was missing from that group and that was Princess Tess. Voltron warned anyone on his ship found aiding her would be put to death instantly. He and Betel had the best trained warriors standing guard outside Voltron's quarters. They were on the engineering deck and transportation deck as well. Betel had made the order to go with full shields on so nobody could invade or fire on the ship. The heightened security made everyone a little tense.

When Lyssa came back to Voltron's quarters she had spoken to him about Vaughn. She told him that originally Vaughn had been in on the plot, but because he couldn't kill her and wanted to return her to her parents Boden had attacked him and knocked him out along with her and then left them on the planet to die. She told Voltron how Vaughn had cared for her and helped find food and water. "I don't think he could have done any of that Voltron if he truly wanted me or you dead."

Storming Voltron paced the floor, "By taking you he committed a crime."

"I know, but please spare him on account of me. If it hadn't been for him I would never had been able to get food or water then the babies and I would have died. Healer Belgorod told me I was very dehydrated and under nourished as it was, so really Voltron Vaughn saved my life." She looked up at her tall warrior husband amazed at his handsome face and beautiful blue eyes rimmed in sliver.

Not wanting to upset her he said he would consider all that she had to say. Until a decision was made Warrior Vaughn would be held in the holding cell.

"Would you like a warm shower?" he asked lifting her from the bed and carrying her to the cleansing chamber and helping her into the cleansing chamber. Sitting her on her feet, he removed her shirt, and then undressed himself. Lifting her he walked into the cleansing stall sitting her on the bench they had made so she could shower. He pressed the button letting the warm water relax her. Looking at his little mate with skin so soft and creamy in colored made his stomach tighten. Kneeling behind her he let his hands slowly roamed over her frame massaging the cleaning solution into her soft skin. Coming around front to her he took each breast one in each hand tenderly washed them. Going lower he washed her rounded abdomen and down to her feet. "Turn around and let me wash you." she said smiling at him. He turned his back to her and knelt she washed his hair and shoulders, down his back to his tightly muscled bottom, gently turning him around she washed his shoulders and strong arms. Letting the shower spray more cleaning solution on him she gently washed his chest running her hands over his finely sculpted muscles and stomach. Stopping before she went lower, seeing that he was highly aroused she decided she would help ease him like she had overheard her mother telling one of her friends. Smiling she thought *this just might be fun*.

Leaning his head into her shoulder he moaned his body shuddering with desire. "Lyssa my love, I love you so much. I want you so very very much," breathing heavily, "we can't I will hurt you and the babies." Smiling she reached around to the panel and hit rinse. As they allowed the cleaning solution to be rinsed off them she pulled him between her open legs and asked him to rise. He did so very wearily, his shaft was level with her mouth and she licked at the head making Voltron moan with desire. Smiling up at him, "I have heard from my mother that there are other ways a woman can pleasure her mate since my pregnant body won't allow us to make love. Let me do that to you." She didn't really wait for him to reply but took him lovingly into her mouth and sucked and tasted him. He was sweet to the taste and she liked it. Cupping his balls in her hands she rubbed them together with one hand while placing the other hand on his shaft pumping him. "Lyssa please, I . . . need . . . you . . . oh by the gods what are you doing to me." She continued her ministrations sucking, licking and moving faster and fasters till she felt him stiffen and his release came quickly. She drank him down licking every drop off of his still hard shaft.

His legs where so wobbly he knelt again in front of her as his breathing slowed, taking her in his arms he went back to their bed and gently laid her down. Lying beside her he kissed her tenderly. She started to giggle, "Oh Voltron I am all wet and now so is the bed." Looking down he realized in his haste to lie beside her he forgot to turn on the pressurized air to dry them. Taking the sheet he dried her with it. Getting up he moved her and took the sheets and threw them on the floor finding new ones under the bed making the bed then he placed her on the clean sheets. Once he was finished he went to the food replicator, "Two roast cremi dinners and two cool waters." Seconds later the dinners appeared in the replicator. Bringing them to the bed he gave a plate to Lyssa, placing his on the floor. He stuffed pillows behind her back to help her sit up. She sat her plate on her large abdomen, grabbing his plate he sat on the bed with his legs crossed.

"Um this is so good. I guess I was hungrier than I thought." She said taking a bite.

"You need to eat more Belgorod said you are so tiny to be feeding you and the three babes."

Looking down at her abdomen she smiled, "Yes but there isn't much room for me to eat much." She lovingly placed her hands on her belly. Smiling at her, "Well we will just have to eat smaller amounts but more often. Does that suit your needs my lady? Please try eating just a little more my love?"

"I just don't have the room Voltron, besides my back is hurting something awful." She grimaced. Seeing that she had only taken a few bites he removed the plate and placed it in the chiller. Turning he said, "For later."

Yawning she stretched, "I am tired of being confined to bed and this room but it is for a good cause. How long before we reach Barax?" She had been confined in Voltron's quarters now it seemed like forever.

"Orin said thirty more days and we should be there." Rising he dressed then brought her a gown to wear. Standing her up, he slipped the gown over her head. The soft pink and sliver gown was his favorite she looked beautiful in it. Lifting her in his arms he headed for the door. "Where are we going?" concern etched in her brow.

"I am taking my wife to the bridge for a little outing, some of the warriors have been so worried about you that this should appease their fears at seeing you." he smiled down at her. He was rewarded with a hug and several kisses.

*   *   *   *

That evening she lay next to Voltron listening to his even breathing remembering the outing to the bridge. It had been so nice to leave this room. Everyone was so solicitous, especially Arielle and Voltron's parents who sat beside her as if to protect her. It had been fun but it wore her out she was so thankful that Voltron could sense her exhaustion. Trying to turn over a sharp pain ripped through her abdomen as fluid rushed from her body. Screaming she lay back down. Voltron had jumped at her sound hitting the light panel he saw water and blood in the bed. "Shouting at MAILS to wake Belgorod and get him to his quarter's stat." Running into the cleansing chamber Voltron brought cleaning cloths out and laid them under Lyssa. Doubling over again she turned frightened eyes to Voltron, "It's too soon the babies are coming." Deciding he couldn't wait for the healer Voltron lifted her and ran through the corridor with her in his arms yelling at the warriors to get out of the way. He fled to the elevator barking "Deck 5." Belgorod was just about to get on the elevator when Voltron rushed forward with a moaning Lyssa.

"What's wrong?"

"Liquid and blood gushed out of her." Lyssa groaned again and Voltron returned his attention to her. "Make it stop she pleaded with him."

"Belgorod, do something?" Voltron shouted at him.

He had Voltron lay her on the bed, he had a hypo dermic injector for pain he quickly put it in her thigh. Pulling the med unit over her body to scan for the heart beats of the babies, he sighed with relief, "Thank the gods and goddesses there are still three heart beats. We will have to deliver her right now Voltron. There is no more room and if she carries them any longer they will all die."

"Do it!" Voltron shouted at the healer." MAILS had notified the whole family but it was Arielle who had come to sick bay to be with his brother. They stepped out of the room as Belgorod worked on Lyssa and the babies. Three sick bay nurses ran into the area to help Belgorod to deliver Lyssa's babies.

Out in the corridor Arielle placed his hand on Voltron's shoulder, "Soon my brother you will be holding your sons and daughter." Nodding Voltron rose to pace back and forth stopping every once in a while to listen at the sick bay door. Pulling on Voltron's arm Arielle forced him to sit. He commed Ea and asked him to bring a grog to sick bay for Voltron. Within minutes Ea was there with the drink.

"Can you sit with him Ea, I am on duty now and I can't stay any longer. I have commed mother and father and told them to wait until the babies were born to come down. However, knowing my mother she will be here soon. Thanks Ea for sitting with him."

Nodding his head yes he sat down next to Voltron and handed him a drink. Voltron took it and looked at it as if he didn't know what to do with it. "She will be fine lad, females give birth every day." Ea spoke. Voltron unconsciously nodded. Hearing Lyssa scream Voltron and Ea paled. Still staring into the drink Ea placed his hand on his shoulder not knowing what to say to his longtime friend. Finally Ea got Voltron to drink the grog but it did nothing to relieve the fear that Voltron was feeling. It seemed like they had sat there for hours. Voltron's mother arrived after a while; she came to sit with her son. "I'll stay with him now Ea. Thanks" she smiled at him.

Sitting quietly Aiofe began singing her prayer for the gods and goddesses to help her new daughter to birth these beautiful little babies that she carried. Hearing his mother's melodious and soft voice Voltron sat down and listened to her. He laid his head back against the wall closing his eyes listening to the beautiful words of his people's song.

Shaking her son awake Aiofe said "Voltron, Voltron, your babies are here and everyone is fine."

Rubbing the sleep from his eyes he jumped up rushing into sick bay. He barely acknowledged the babies as he hurried pass them to where Lyssa lay, she was so pale and her eyes were closed. Kneeling beside the bed he picked up her hand, "please don't leave me Lyssa? I can't raise our babies without you." he voice caught as he pictured his life without her.

"Voltron, she is fine, I gave her a sedative to sleep." Belgorod said. "She worked really hard at delivering these babies of yours. She is a strong woman. Most women would have given up hours ago." Taking the rag and moping his brow again he spoke, "She wouldn't let me give her any pain medicine, she was afraid it would hurt the babies."

As Voltron listened to Belgorod his heart swelled with pride in his mate, he heard a tiny mewling sound. Look up Belgorod asked smiled, "Would you like to see your children?"

Rising he went over to the neonatal units to see them. "They are so small," turning to Belgorod he asked, "are you sure they are alright?"

"Yes they are fine, but they will be staying in the sick bay for a while till they get a little bigger. Baby Alpha weighed in at three pounds, Baby Beta weighed in at three pounds, Baby Gamma weighed in at two pounds eight ounces."

Looking at the babies he marveled at how the boys were so like him and Lyssa each had dark blue/black hair with golden highlights. The baby girl had pure blonde with highlights of blue/black. They were beautiful. Lyssa had given him strong babies even if they were only a nano parsec big. Taking a deep breath Voltron sat on the chair next to the units that housed his babies.

"Voltron go to your room and rest. I promise as soon as Lyssa wakes I will have MAILS awaken you." Belgorod urged.

"I want to be here when she wakes."

"I know you do but you will do her better if you rest so you can take care of her and the babies when they are strong enough to go to your quarters." Seeing the logic in that statement, he rose went to Lyssa and kissed her on the forehead. Caressing her cheek he smiled down at her with a deeper love that he didn't even realize he had until now. Leaving he went to his quarters. Not even undressing he flopped on the bed and was a sleep even before his head hit the pillow.

Arriving at Barax for the Galactic Athnam the Erne docked at the planets space station. Lyssa sat in their new quarters as the men had removed one of the walls between two sleeping quarters to make room for the babies. The babies each weighed in at four pounds and were growing daily they were now thirty one days old. Aiofe was sitting with Lyssa and feeding one of the babies an enriched nutrient milk substitute. Aiofe smiled down at little Teagan who was eating faster than the boys. "Slow down little one," Aiofe giggled as Teagan looked up and cooed at her.

"They sure are hungry a lot. I find myself getting up three times a night just to make sure they are eating enough." Laughed Lyssa, "Voltron has offered to get up with them but I always feel so bad since he has returned full time to the bridge," she said with a yawn. "When will be going to the surface for the Council meeting?"

"Zephron has told me that he and the boys will attend the preliminary meeting today at twenty one hundred hours. When they return they will have the schedule of the Athnam and we will see when we are on the list to announce our concerns about Boden and Vaughn and the war they nearly started" Lifting Teagan to burp her Aiofe continued, "We received a message that your father and mother will be here for dinner tonight. It will be good to see them and I am sure they are anxious to see you and these precious babies." Rising she laid Teagan down to sleep. "Well I must return and ready myself for the dinner tonight, do you have any special requests?" she asked Lyssa.

"Well yes, I would like to have roast cremi on the menu. I have come to love that dish."

Laughing Aiofe bent and kissed her daughter "I will see if Ea can prepare that as well." Turning she picked up Rylan and handed him to his mother. Leaving she blew a kiss at her beautiful grandchildren.

After feeding Rylan she laid him down next to his twin brother, after tucking them in she went to the cleansing chamber to shower and ready herself for the return of Voltron and the dinner festivities.

"Secretary Pelee." said the Galactic magistrate as he banged his gavel down to regain order, "remain seated. We have a slot for all to speak about their concerns of the war that went on between Zarift and Zephron"

"How can we be sure that King Zarift and King Zephron will even attend this Athnam?" The Secretary from Pleightese asked. Sitting higher up in the stadium sat King Zephron who was fuming, *how dare that snarck Pelee acted like he wasn't even there.* King Zephron started to rise. Voltron placed his hand on his father's leg. "Do not rise to the bait father. All will come out." Feeling a little chagrined at being told by his son to calm down Zephron grunted. "If, you say so, my son."

"Now if we can continue with the Athnam agenda without further interruptions we shall proceed." The head of the Galactic Council said.

King Zephron, Prince Voltron, Prince Tiernan, Prince Arielle walked from the stadium to catch the next space shuttle back to the Erne. "Did you see the son of a galactic snarck Duke Killian sitting at the council bench with the Galactic Council?" Tiernan spit out. "Who does he think he is?"

"I found it odd as well. Usually a Duke does not sit on the council yet he acted like he was a part of the council full time. What do you think of it father?" both Tiernan and Voltron asked at the same time.

"It has never been done. Usually the seats on the council are for the royalty and he certainly is not royalty. Makes me wonder what Magistrate Kingston is doing?"

The ride to the ship was done so in quite as each man was thinking on the events at the meeting. Once on board Voltron went directly to his quarters. He had less than an hours to prepare for their dinner guest.

Lyssa was humming to the babies and did not hear Voltron come in. He watched her as she lifted each baby and kissed them tenderly and sang just to them. He could hear the cooing and the soft giggling of each of his babies. He was amazed at how his love had grown for Lyssa. He had never wanted to mate again but she had changed all that. She had given him the love he had wanted from Elena and the loyalty he thought he had from Elena. Now he realized that he never had that from her. She continued to sing picking up Teagan she spun around cooing and singing stopping short when she saw Voltron standing in the doorway watching her. Turning she laid Teagan down tucking her blanket around her. Going to Rylan and Brylan she did the same. Turning she looked at him with passion filled eyes, "Do you see anything you like sir?" she asked teasingly, lifting her skirt above her knee.

His breath caught in his throat. He had not touched her in so long that his need for her rose immediately and she saw the results of her teasing. Walking to her he spoke huskily, "Yes I do my lady. I see a comely wench with blonde hair spun like gold." Reaching her he lifted her into his arms, sniffing her hair he buried his face in her neck. Placing kisses along her neck to her jaw he finally reached her lips and spoke before placing the kiss, "I need you my wife, my love my Lyssa. I need the love you give me and only me you are mine, mine for all time." Kissing her passionately she forgot all about the dinner they were going to and melted into his embrace.

"Oh Voltron, I love you with my whole heart, my soul and my body. As I am yours you are mine, mine to touch, to kiss to love. I need you my husband I need your hands touching me loving me, I need your lips on mine." She breathed into his mouth.

Letting go of her legs she slide down his frame feeling the evidence of his arousal. Molding into him she placed her arms around his waist and brought him closer to her. Just as their kiss was deepening the com buzzed. "Commander Voltron, you are wanted on the bridge." Pulling away from her he slammed on the button of the com, "This had better damn well be an emergency." He bellowed in the com.

"Sorry sir, King Zarift has asked you to join him on the bridge."

Placing his head on the wall above the com he tried to calm his aroused body he hit the button again. "I will be there in fifteen minutes Voltron out." Turning to Lyssa he caught her smiling behind her hand. He then snickered as well. "When this damn Athnam is done our mothers are going to watch our off springs so we can have a honeymoon."

"Only a honeymoon is it?" she smiled, "I was hoping for at least two. I need to go and repair my hair that you damaged in your aroused state." She grinned.

He hated to leave her but her father was a King and deserved to be treated with honor and respect even if he did interrupt their passion filled kiss. Adjusting his pants he ran his hands through his hair, taking a deep breath he said, "I will return to get you before dinner." Then he was gone.

"I don't care what the Intel says; Calum was in on this as well." King Zarift said

"How do you know this?" Tiernan asked unbelieving.

Speaking up Voltron said, "It doesn't matter anyway, Calum is dead and Vaughn is in a holding cell on the Talisman. But continue Zarift at least we only have one warrior to find."

Zarift went on with what he knew, "They were at my country home where my daughter Tess was staying. Warrior Finn saw them and just reported it to me otherwise I would have told you sooner. When he saw Calum, Vaughn and Boden he hid himself and listened at the window, he kept hidden till he thought they were gone when he heard another man's voice with Tess. It was that bastard Killian. Finn heard that they were planning to take over my kingdom and yours. They do not like that you have complete power over the Zephron gems. Their plan is to try and kill us at the Athnam." King Zarfit sat down, "Tess wanted Lyssa dead as well, apparently Boden and Vaughn where charged with fulfilling that request."

Voltron slammed his hand down on the railing. "By the gods and goddesses I will see Boden killed. To think they almost cost me my mate and my children." He raged on.

"I think I can get a private meeting with the Magistrate he has asked me on several occasion to get some very hush, hush, Intel on his wife. I think he owes me one don't you?" Tiernan grinned, "After dinner I will send him a private message."

Aiofe came from her room and stated that dinner was ready in the private dinning galley. Voltron went back and got Lyssa and made sure the young nurse from sick bay was there to watch the triplets while they were gone. He also had security set outside their quarters, he was taking no chances. Arlana and Arielle came once they were off duty. King Zarift and Queen Zephorah arrived just as Voltron and Lyssa entered the dinning gallery.

Smiling Lyssa said, "Yum something smells delicious."

"I agree." Said Tiernan

They all nodded their heads in agreement. Ea came in from the private cooking chamber and placed the meal on the table. Once that was done he went around and poured everyone a cup of infused café beans and cocoa beans, it smelled delicious.

Taking a sip, Lyssa asked Ea "Where did this come from?"

"From a supply ship that brought goods from the Milky Way Galaxy, they say it is grown on a planet called earth."

"Um it has a delicious flavor I like it." She smiled. Everyone agreed that the taste was delicious.

Turning to her parents she lifted the plate of roast cremi to them, "Try this you are going to love the flavor. It is one of Voltron's favorite and now mine." She said smiling.

Once the meal was underway the topic of conversation turned to the war and the stealing of the gems. "I just don't understand what Tess hoped to gain in her evil plan. I knew she didn't love her sister but I had no idea she hated her to the point of wanting her dead." Zarifts voice broke speaking of his girls.

Going to him Lyssa knelt in front of him, "Father I am so sorry, I know you love Tess. Even though she wants me dead I still love her. Her mother's hatred of you twisted her thinking where you are concerned," rising she put her arms around his neck, "I know you loved her as much as you loved me. Don't blame yourself for her evil minded ways." Hugging her back King Zarift cleared his throat and wiped his eyes, embarrassed at his tears. Queen Zephorah placed her hand lovingly on his arm and squeezed it. "It will be alright Zarift we will get through this together." Zarift patted her hand lovingly. "Well," replied Zarift before I retire for the night I would like to look upon my grandsons and granddaughter." Rising he took Zephorah's hand went to nursery to see his grandchildren.

"I'll be right there mom and dad." Turning to Queen Aiofe and King Zephron "would you like to come and say good night to them as well?" she smiled.

"Yes." They rose and went as well. Leaning down she gave Voltron a kiss that held many promises. "Don't stay too late with Tiernan and Arielle." She said smiling. "Arlana come with me so you can see the babies." Rising Arlana went to her and followed her to the nursery.

It felt like many hours later that Voltron entered their quarters. He was tired and wore out trying to find Boden. It was as if he had disappeared from the universe. Before he went to the cleansing chamber he turned to go to the nursery. He found Lyssa there humming to the babies. Going to her he took Rylan from her arms and kissed his little cheek. Laying him in his cradle he turned and pickup Teagan giving her a kiss on her little cheek then laid her down for the night. Brylan was a little fussier so Voltron took him from Lyssa and told her to go ready herself for bed. He would rock and feed Brylan and then he would be in.

An hour later Voltron walked into the bedroom, taking his clothes off and throwing them in the sanitizer he turned to see if Lyssa was a sleep, she wasn't in the bed and wondered where she was. Stretching he headed for the shower. Walking into the cleansing chamber his breath caught as Lyssa stood there naked before him. Her body was beautiful. Letting her hair down she beckoned for him to join her in the shower. As he looked at her he couldn't believe how beautiful she was. Having the babies only made her curvier her breast were larger and rounder now, something he found exciting. Walking to her he started breathing hard; he had missed not being able to mount her. He had wanted her to heal after the babies and he didn't mind waiting. His reward for waiting was standing naked and beautiful before him now.

He walked into the shower completely aroused and Lyssa's heart stuttered as he stood before her. She had missed him the long weeks after the birth of the babies she couldn't believe how patient and loving he had been. The birth had been hard and Belgorod insisted that she wait the required 4 weeks. She had patiently waited and so had Voltron, but now the waiting was over and they could once again enjoy the pleasures of their love making.

Washing each other, they took their time re-exploring each other's bodies. His need for her was growing, kissing her touching her was almost more than he could take; lifting her by her waist she wrapped her legs around him. She was eager for his rigid shaft to thrust into her wet sheath. In his eagerness he slammed her hard against the wall, reaching for his rigid cock she took it and guided into her. He moaned as he thrust deep into. She arched her back so he could suck on her nipples. Taking her mouth they both eagerly deepened the kiss. Turning with her he walked to the bed where he placed them both on the bed never losing contact with her. His thrusts quickened, she felt her release nearing wrapping her legs securely around his waist she bucked her hips reveling in the liquid gold feeling her release brought her.

He made sure she had her release first Voltron rolled over with her onto his back letting her ride him. He watched as her breasts bobbed with her up and down movements. Leaning forward she once again offered her breasts to his questing mouth. His cock pulled deliciously on her inner flesh causing ripples of pleasure to run down her spine and into her very core. He grabbed the sheets at the intensity of her movements. He knew he couldn't hold on much longer. Grabbing her waist, he rolled her over on to her back and pumped faster and faster; nearing his release he bent and bit her flesh on her shoulder, kissing and licking it sending waves of pleasure through her once more. With one final thrust, he released his seed deep into her warm and waiting body. Resting on his elbows he rolled to the side of her both of them completely satisfied. They both lay still breathing hard. Finally their breathing returned to normal. Looking down at his beautiful sexy wife he pulled her to him and kissed her gently. Easing into him she kissed him back sighing satisfied.

"You love me well my lover, my warrior." She said softly.

"As you do me my love my wife. I was so happy to see you waiting for me in the shower tonight. I was afraid you were going to be a sleep when I got back. I don't think I could have waited one more night to touch you." he said holding her close.

"I know my love our little ones have certainly taken some of our time away from each other so I asked Gennie to stay tonight to feed the babies when they wake and she smiled and said yes. So

I am yours all night long if you wish?" She looked seductively.

Rolling over on top of her he began kissing her again evidence of his wanting her poking her in the thigh. Kissing his lips she said to him, "Roll over warrior I want to taste you again."

"If you insist my lady." He said huskily.

He rolled over and allowed her to take him into her mouth. Licking, sucking and rubbing his turgid shaft she stopped and took his ball sack into her mouth. He moaned and bucked his hips he almost felt that he would die from her touch. Gasping he said, "By the gods and goddesses Lyssa you make me weak in my knees." They made love all through the night falling asleep just before the morning alarm went off. Gennie gently rapped on the bedroom door, grabbing her robe Lyssa went to the door. "Yes Gennie is everything alright?"

"Yes my princess, it just that I am on duty in less than an hour." She noticed how tired Lyssa was and half smiled knowing that the prince had kept her up long last night.

"Ok Gennie just let me put on some clothes and I be there soon." Smiling at Gennie starting to turn looked over her shoulder, "I want to thank you for staying last night."

"I was my pleasure princess." Gennie said shyly.

Going into the cleansing chamber Lyssa took a quick shower and dressed as quietly as possible she didn't want Voltron to wake. Combing her long hair she left it down and went into the baby's nursery. Already Brylan and Rylan where making their demands known, Teagan was just lying there listening to her brothers wailing. Picking up Brylan Lyssa grabbed the bottle of milk, Gennie had called Queen Aiofe and she had arrived to help feed the babies as well.

Sitting in the rocking chair feeding Brylan, Aiofe took Rylan and sat in the other rocking chair feed him his morning bottle. Looking at Lyssa Aiofe spoke, "You look beautiful today Lyssa. What did you do to your hair?" she asked.

Scrunching up her face she smiled, "I have just left my hair down my lady."

"Stop with my lady Lyssa, you are my daughter and I love you and these babies that you have given us. Please call me mother." Aiofe smiled back

Finishing Brylan's morning bottle, Lyssa changed his diaper and placed him in his cradle. Going to Teagan she got another bottle and started feeding her. "You are such a patient baby Teagan, yes you are," Lyssa smiled and cooed at

Teagan. "Your brothers on the other hand demand to be fed first, those boys are going to grow big and strong and they will protect you as their little sister. Always remember that Teagan your brothers will always be there for you." She said lifting Teagan and kissing her gently on her check. Teagan cooed and smiled at her mother.

Voltron had finally awakened and came into the room to find his mother and his beautiful mate taking care of his babies. He had heard what Lyssa had said to Teagan. Going to her he picked her up and kissed her on her cheek as well, "That's right my little daughter, your brothers will always be there for you. Now go to sleep and grow big and strong like your mother." Lying Teagan back down, he tucked her blanket around her. Kissing Lyssa on the cheek he turned and kissed his mother on her cheek. "Well I am going to the bridge. Why don't you call Ea and ask him to bring you and mother a pot of that wonderful café bean and cocoa drink to wake you?" he said smiling devilishly.

"I may just do that." She smiled at him as she yawned. "Voltron before you go when are we slotted to go to the Athnam?" she asked.

"I think father said we were on the schedule for fifteen hundred hours. Why?"

"I wanted to make sure one of the nurses can stay with the babies while we are at the Athnam." She said.

"That's fine I will be back in plenty of time to have dinner and bathe before we go." Waving he left the nursery going to the bridge.

Aiofe and Lyssa finished feeding the babies and they were sleeping so Lyssa called Ea to ask if he could bring some of that café bean and cocoa drink. Sitting and talking it was nice to have Voltron's mother as a friend and ally. Alyssa commed her mother and asked her join them for some of this new beverage that Ea had introduced them to.

*　　*　　*　　*

Tess sat down next to Boden waiting for Killian to arrive. Boden was restless, rising he went to the food panel and ordered a grog turning he spoke to Tess, "Would you like one?" he asked

"Yes" she nodded at him.

Killian walked through the door and asked Boden to get him a drink as well. Bringing the drinks to the table Boden sat down.

"The Zephron's and the Zarifts will be meeting with the galactic counsel at fifteen hundred hours. That gives us one hour twenty minutes to ready ourselves for the deaths of the Zephron and Zarift royalty and our takeover of their houses." Lifting his cup, he saluted Boden and Tess and grinned evilly. *Soon I will be the only one to rule both houses, once I get rid of Tess I will have all that I have desired.*

"I have the blast charges hidden under the galactic council's benches. It took long enough to do this I guess there was a last minute change and the Athnam committee had a few last minute changes for the arena floor plan. The charges are under the table where the Zephron and Zarifts will be sitting as wekk." Boden said.

"Good," Killian said, "There can be no mistakes when the council, Zephron's and the Zarifts are killed. I will not be sitting at the council bench but I will be meeting with the lower council getting agenda items ready for the rest of the Athnam. With me out of the way no one will suspect that I have had any part in this plot." He smiled evilly at Tess, "I need you out of Barax before this goes down. I do not want any one putting you and me together until we are ready to reveal our plan. Do I make myself clear Tess?" he asked sneering.

I hate Killian, I know that after this all goes down the he will try and get rid of me. Keeping control of her emotions, she spoke lovingly at him, "Yes Killian my love, I plan on telling everyone that I will be on Morgana at a spa there. I will be waiting to hear from you when this is all over." Smiling so sweetly at him that she thought she was going to retch.

"Boden, after you have detonated the devices follow us to Kian." Tess said.

"Aye Princes Tess I will meet you there as soon as I am done." Leaving he remained hidden until the council meeting at fifteen hundred hours.

*   *   *   *

It was the time for the Zephron's and Zarifts to attend the Athnam. They all rode together in the space shuttle. Landing at the space dock Voltron put a protective arm around Lyssa. Waiting at the space dock a jitney arrived to take them to the arena where the Athnam was being held. Sitting there in their seats were the entire planetary councils members. Taking the hover pad to their level the Zephron's sat down and waited for the Zarifts to arrive at their level of seating. Banging the gavel, Magistrate Jungpa called the Athnam to order. "Please rise for the council pledge." The entire arena rose to honor the pledge that their ancestors had made centuries ago.

Sitting down Magistrate Jungpa spoke clear and loud, "I now call before the council the royal house of Zephron and the royal house of Zarift."

Underneath the stadium where the council sat Boden waited for the group to approach the bench. His hands were sweaty and he shook knowing that if this didn't work he would be on the run for the rest of his life. If it worked he would be able to live a life of wealth on a distant planet.

King Zephron, Queen Aiofe, King Zarift, Queen Zephorah along with Prince Voltron, Princess Lyssa and Prince Tiernan road the hover pad to the magistrate's bench. Noticeably missing was Duke Killian from the bench. Scowling Voltron did not understand anyway how the spurious unethical spawn of hell had wormed his way onto the council bench. The hover pad stopped directly in front of the magistrate.

Bowing his head King Zephron spoke, your honor the house of Zephron comes before you with . . . ," at that moment Boden pushed the detonator button. He had approximately ten minutes to leave the area before he was killed along with the Zephron's, Zarifts and the Magistrate and council.

"There had been a marriage proposal that would have made an alliance between the house of Zephron and the house of Zarifts. With this alliance we would begin sharing the gems of Zephron and the technology that was needed for space travel and as a galactic weapon. We are unsure why . . ." the blast had destroyed the bench where the magistrate had sat, the hover crafts were blown up in to the arena. Hearing the blast Boden left smiling to himself for his great success.

The magistrate, his council and the Zephron's and Zarifts were transported safely from Boden and Tess' evil plot. "Welcome aboard Prince Voltron."

"Thanks Warrior Bryce. Are there any injured from the blast?" he asked.

"No, because of the warning the hall engineers had placed the bench farther away from the seats in the arena. They had also put up blast proof glass." Bryce answered.

Taking the transport elevator to the bridge Voltron hugged Lyssa and told her to go to their children. His mother followed Lyssa as the men went to the bridge.

"A communication has just gone out stating that the magistrate, the council and the house of Zephron and the house of Zarift have been killed by a blast at the Athnam." Arielle replied.

"The word has gone out that the Talisman and the Erne housing the last of the house of Zephron is going into hiding until authorities get to the bottom of this atrocity." Taking a breath Arielle went on. "Authorities on Zarift are looking for Princess Tess in order to protect her."

The group was grim as they turned to go to their quarters when the com link came on Lyssa screamed, "Voltron our babies are gone!" she cried hysterically. "Voltron, where are you I need . . ."

Running from the bridge Voltron shot into the elevator and yelled Deck 4. Rushing into the room he found Aiofe holding Lyssa as she continued to sob. Taking her into his arms his heart broke at her tears. "Lyssa we will find our children." He spoke softly.

Shaking her head no she cried out, "Tess is behind this. She hates me and doesn't want me to be happy. Oh Voltron our little babies are gone and probably so afraid." Rising she raged on, "I am going to kill her when I find her."

"Lyssa do you trust me and love me?" he question softly holding her at arms link and looking deeply in her eyes.

She took a deep breath and nodded, "I trust and I love you more than life itself."

"Then we together will find our babies." He said with determination. "Where is the sick bay nurse that was staying with them?" he asked.

"She wasn't here when we arrived." Aiofe said.

Hitting the com link he said, "Belgorod where is the nurse that was attending the babies while we were gone?"

"She is in your quarters."

"No she is not. Please come to my quarters immediately, Voltron out."

Zephron, Zarift and his wife came into Voltron's quarters. Zephorah was crying, Zarift attempting to console her. Zephron went to Aiofe and led her to the couch to sit. Voltron had taken Lyssa into their room and sat her on the bed asking his parents to send Belgorod into them when he arrived.

He was holding and rocking Lyssa when Belgorod got there. "When did we get the nurse Kara?" Voltron asked.

"She came shortly after the attack on Varian. She had just graduated from the academy. You don't think she has been bought do you?" Belgorod asked incredulously.

"She was left in charge of the babies while we were at the Athnam. Lyssa were the guards at the door when you arrived?" Voltron asked.

Looking up through her red-rimmed eyes, she shook her head no, "I didn't even think about them not being outside our door."

"Arthur, where are the warriors that were on guard duty this afternoon outside my quarters?"

"They should still be there." Arthur said.

"They are gone and I want them found."

"Aye Voltron I will find them."

Voltron hit the com link again, "Bryce were there any unauthorized transportation bay departures?" he asked.

"Not on my watch. Commander "However, Junior Warrior Vincent was on duty before me. I will ask him."

Bryce came to Voltron's quarters with warrior Vincent in tow along with Arthur dragging his security warriors with him. Throwing Vincent into the room, he landed on the floor before Commander Voltron. Jumping to his feet Voltron grabbed Vincent by the throat rage pulsing through his body. "What have you done?" He clenched his fist by his side ready to kill him. The security warriors backed up considerable paler at what they witnessed.

Cowering, Vincent hung his head, "Commander she told me you had ordered her to take the babies to the Athnam to show off the future house of Zephron. I had no idea she was intending to kidnap them." He pleaded.

Seeing his fear Lyssa stood up placing a hand on Voltron's arm. He turned to look at her. What he saw in her eyes surprised him. "Voltron, it is not Warrior Vincent's fault, this is the work of Tess. Please release him. You are treating him unjustly and I for one think he can help us trace her departure."

Dropping Vincent, Voltron grabbed her, "By the gods and goddesses you are right my love. I was so filled with rage that I didn't think about the trace of the transport pod."

"Commander she did not leave by the transportation pod, she left in a skimmer."

Voltron's rage and anger finally broke and he turned unleashing it on the young warrior. Picking him up by the throat he pummeled him in the face. It took Warrior Bryce, King Zephron and King Zarift to pull the distraught Voltron off the young Warrior. Arthur turned to his security guards, "Why did you leave your posts?"

"We had a com-link from Commander Voltron saying we could stand down." The warriors swallowed waiting to see if Voltron was going to attack them as he had Vincent.

Lyssa anger was no less volatile but she wanted answers. Going to the bridge she spoke to Tiernan. "Can you find the skimmers trace?" she asked Tiernan.

"Yes I have been listening in on your quarters I am already on it Lyssa." He smiled at her. "I have ready Voltron's skimmer. When you are ready to go so are we."

Hitting the bridge com Lyssa spoke, "Voltron, Belgorod, Betel, Tiernan, Arthur and father meet me in the transportation bay. We are going after our babies."

Tiernan's crew feed the coordinate to the skimmer, with Voltron in the commanders seat with Lyssa next to him they left the docking bay.

The coordinates where not unfamiliar to them, "Just as I thought the criminals have returned to the crime scene."

Time passed slowly as the skimmer made its way to Kian, the whole way Lyssa prayed to the gods and the goddesses that their babies where alright. Getting up from her seat she paced in the back of skimmer not able to stay seated.

"We are within two hundred lengths from the planet." Spoke Tiernan as he began preparing the skimmer to for landed. Hitting the galactic position module Tiernan quickly found where the skimmer had landed. Choosing a coordinate about a hundred yards away they sat down. Belgorod strapped his pack onto this back. It was filled with meds, nutrition and a med scanner to check the babies once they were found. Betel, Tiernan strapped on the stun grenades setting them at the lowest level possible in order to not hurt the babies if they were being held by the kidnappers. Voltron took his grandfather's sword and strapped it to his belt. Lyssa took her sword as well and placed it in the sheath down her back. She had changed into her battle garb. Looking at each other with a nod Betel and Tiernan left the skimmer first. Scanning the area there were no life signs near the other craft. Carefully walking the short distant to the skimmer they searched the ground for foot prints. Luckily for them there had been no storms to disturb the prints left behind. Following the prints they soon came upon the kidnappers. Sitting in a circle around a fire sat, Boden, Kara and Tess. Tess was holding the babies snuggling them to her body. Betel and Tiernan were able to get nearer while Voltron, Lyssa and Belgorod moved to the left of them hoping to catch them off guard.

Boden stooped to stir the fire he had made a make-shift tent to keep the babies in from the stormy weather that Kian was known for. "How long before they figure out that the babies are gone?"

Shaking her head at the stupid warrior Tess looked at Boden, "By the gods and goddesses Boden are you truly that stupid?" she sneered.

Rising he threw the branch down tired of this bitch constantly treating him like a commoner. If he didn't have the gems any more he would kill her he so despised her. Turning he stormed off if he stayed near her one Nano sec longer he would kill her.

Kara looked up at Tess they had been friends a long time. Of course Kara had been in service to the royal house and their friendship was not encouraged. Getting up she moved next to Tess putting her arm around her. Smiling she said, "They are truly beautiful aren't they?"

"Um they are. I had no idea I would like them this much? "Tess said as she stroked Rylan's cheek.

"You know it is time for their feeding do you want to help me?" she asked. Rising Kara went to the make-shift tent and pulled out the pack containing the nutrient enriched milk and gave a feeder to Tess for Rylan as she took one for Teagan.

Lyssa's heart clenched as she saw her sisters hands on her babies. Her heart started beating so fast that Lyssa thought she was going to pass out. Rising she started to take her sword from her sheath as Voltron stopped her. Putting his finger to his lips he shook his head no. Pointing just beyond them he saw Boden standing next to a grove of bent twisted trees. Looking Lyssa saw Boden as well. She understood what Voltron wanted and started crawling away from Voltron and around to where Boden stood.

"Bring me Brylan I will feed him as well."

"You do seem to love the little princes." Kara said as she brought Brylan to Tess. Sitting next to her Kara wrapped her arm around Tess and began caressing her shoulder. Tess leaned into her and then turned her waiting lips for Kara to kiss. It was just the distraction they needed to attack the group. Lyssa standing up quickly brought the sword down killing Boden before Boden knew she was there. Running to the fire Voltron kicked Kara out of the way as he turned toward Tess who was still holding Brylan. Jumping up from the ground Kara ran head long hitting Voltron square in the back propelling him forward. Still clinging to him she tried to grab the sword from his waist.

Jumping up Tess grab Rylan and started running toward the skimmer. Belgorod had gone back to the skimmer waiting for the word that they had the babies. Tiernan watched as Tess grabbed Rylan and started running. He started forward but then saw Lyssa sprinting after her sister. Almost getting to the skimmer Lyssa screamed at Tess. "Stop Tess, you have my children!" she said boldly as Tess stopped and turned slowly toward her sister. Holding Rylan and Brylan she stood defiantly staring at Lyssa. "Yes, they are your children and they are beautiful." She said in tight voice.

"Give them to me Tess I know you don't want to hurt them?"

Laughing evilly Tess raised the twin boys and kissed each one on their cheek, "You know I always envied you Lyssa. Father always loved you the best." She sneered. "My mother hated him, and she left me because she could not stand being near him. I never knew the loving father like you did." She spoke quietly rubbing the twins little arms with her thumb as she spoke.

It had taken Voltron no time to kill Kara he hadn't batted an eye. Killing a woman this time was justified she had tried to tear his family apart. Turning he ran after Lyssa.

"You know I would have married Voltron I was going to try and change my life but as always you ruined it for me." Laying the babies down Tess stepped away from them and drew the sword she had strapped to her waist. Raising it she rushed Lyssa. Lyssa sidestepped her sister hitting Tess across her back. Tess screamed out in pain.

Tiernan had been watching from a distance and as soon as Tess had placed the twins on the ground, he ran and grabbed the babies out of harm's way. Betel had taken Teagan back to Belgorod where Tiernan met them handing the babies over to the healer to scan.

"Tess I don't want to kill you, please stop and I will make sure you are taken care of."

Laughing maniacally "Lyssa you little stupid idiot, do you think I care if you get me help. I have killed your Voltron, his family, and our family. It is you who will need help from me?" She stood sword held out front of her. Lyssa circled her slowly laughing just as cruelly, "You think you have killed my family our family? You are so delusional Tess. Turn around and look for yourself Voltron stand just in back of you."

The smile fell from her face as she quickly turned seeing Voltron she screamed and rushing him with her blade high in the air.

"Voltron, don't kill her." Lyssa yelled.

Stepping out of the way he put out his leg and tripped her. Rolling over she eyed Voltron angrily, "As we stand here fighting warrior, Duke Killian is closing the deal and having the galactic council name him successor of Zephron and Zarift." Rising from the ground she wiped the sweat from her forehead with her sleeve.

Rushing to Voltron's side she heard what Tess was saying. She started to laugh and gave her sister a smug smile, "Tess you are delusional, we were aware of your treachery and managed to have Warrior Bryce transported our families and the magistrate and council up to the Erne. You were defeated even before you started this plan."

Screaming her rage Tess turned quickly and ran from Voltron and Lyssa. Betel and Tiernan both started after her but Voltron halted their progress. "Leave her." Grabbing Lyssa they went to their skimmer where Belgorod was cooing and talking to the three babies.

"You are growing so strong. Yes you are. Your mother and father are so proud of you my princes' and princess." Tickling their chubby little cheeks all three cooed out their approval. Turning he saw that everyone had witnessed his play with the babies. Shrugging his shoulders he quirked his mouth, "They are so cute what can I say?"

"Are they well?" Lyssa went to the babies gather them in her arms. Voltron was right there as well taking his whole family into his arms.

Smiling Belgorod said, "Yes, they weathered their ordeal quite well princess."

Tears streamed down her cheeks as she hugged her babies and leaned into her husband. "Let's leave this place before a storm comes."

Back on the Erne everyone was so solicitous of the babies and their mom. Ea had prepared a special dinner of roast cremi for Voltron and Lyssa. Aiofe insisted on keeping the babies with her in the nursery so that Voltron and Lyssa could rest. Tiernan, Arielle, Arlana had stayed to help Aoife with the babies and King Zephron went to his quarters alone yet happy. King Zarift and Zephorah went to their quarters to mourn their daughter Tess. Security was on full alert again. There would be no mistakes this time. If Tess somehow got off Kian and found Killian and thought they could hurt his family again it was just not going to happen.

Lying next to Lyssa Voltron rubbed her arm as he held her. Reaching up to her husband she caressed his cheek. "I love you so very much Voltron, you are my love and my warrior."

"I love you. You and our babies are my life now. I had no idea how much one person could love. You have given me everything I thought I had lost." Rolling toward her he captured her lips and kissed her deeply. Sighing she snuggled closer to this man that have given her everything she had always wanted in life.

CHAPTER SIX

Finding Tess and Duke Killian

$\mathcal{I}$t had been three months since the incident on Kian. During that time, the babies had grown substantially. Tiernan and Voltron had followed several dead ended leads as to the whereabouts of Killian and Tess. Returning from one such lead Voltron came into their room to find his children lying in their beds. Lyssa sat reading a story to them. Hearing Voltron enter the room all three babies turned their head and sat up in bed, "Dada, dada, dada," they all three said.

Smiling at them he kissed each one on the top of their heads. "When did they start speaking?" he asked going to Lyssa to kiss her.

"A couple of weeks ago, they are saying mama, dada, papa, gamma. They are so cute. Alright you three time for sleep." Rising she went to them and kissed them and tucked them in. Taking Voltron by the arm she led him to their sleep chamber. Going to him she hugged him around the waist. She rose up on her toes to kiss his lips. Her lips were gentle at first but soon became very demanding.

Growling Voltron lifted her up and lay her on the bed. Stripping her clothes from her he quickly undressed. Falling down on top of her he sought her lips while his hands roamed over her curves. Inhaling he moaned at the assault on his senses. Opening her legs for him she wrapped them around his waist feeling his hard shaft waiting for entrance into her warm recesses.

Her hands explored his body, moaning as she grasped his bottom and felt him stiffen with desire. "I want you Voltron." She spoke huskily.

Rising up with her he locked her in his arms as he turned over and laid her on top of him. His shaft pulsed at her opening the head of him pushing against her demanding entrance. Rising above him she took his shaft and guided him into her. Groaning he arched his back pushing deeper into her. Splaying her hands across his chest she massaged his muscles reveling in the feel of him. She rode him till he could take it no more grabbing her hips he rolled over to thrust deeper into her. She rode the wave of pleasure letting Voltron take her to new heights in his love making. Pumping faster Voltron bent down and trailed kisses down her cheek to the soft area of her neck. Feeling his release near he bit down on her causing her to once more reach her release, his release came quickly they rode the wave of passion together. Lying beside her his breathing finally returned to normal. Wrapping his arms around her he kissed her again. "I love you so much."

"I love you too my love." Pulling the covers over them they both feel asleep peacefully.

It had been a long and unproductive search for Tess and Killian. They had gone back to Zarift and search the three moons that orbited the planet. From there they had returned to Kian but there was no sign of them any were. Wanted posters had gone out with their pictures stating their crime and if found to contact the Zephronian magistrate to have them extracted back to Zephron.

Voltron and Lyssa doted on their children. Each day the boys grew tall. Healer Belgorod had taken a great interest in the triplets. He and MAILS were studying their DNA. It seemed that with Voltron's bite and Lyssa's fertility they had produced super children. Rylan was already a telepath and an empathy; Brylan and Teague were destined to be great warriors. Their growth rates were so tremendous that at the age of 9 months they functioned more like sixteen month olds. Their development of vocabulary and thought stunned Belgorod. If they continued to grow at the rate, they were growing then by a year they would be two and two they would be four. They were actually doubling in their growth.

Lyssa came into Voltron's study, "The plans for the celebration meal are underway. All the dignitaries are here and the gala kicks off tonight with a royal ball." Looking up from his paper work he motioned for Lyssa to sit on his lap. Taking her into his arms he kissed her. She returned his kiss eagerly and soon the passion ignited between them pulling the hem of her shirt up Voltron sought to caress her breasts. She soon felt the object of his desire and she wiggled around on his stiff shaft and elicited a groan from him.

"Woman you do not play fair," he spoke huskily. Smiling she took his face into her hands, "Warrior I have no idea what you are talking about." She smiled at him looking him straight in his eyes. Growling he kissed her lips again then trailed his kisses down her neck to the soft part of her nape and bit down. As she groaned, he growled with desire and laughed. "Now princess who is playing unfair?" Playfully swatting at him she unbuttoned her bodice and allowed him to suck on her already hard nipples. Moaning softly as he did. He continued to suck as his hand lifted the hem of her dress and slide up to her leg and then to her woman hood. Opening her legs she'd given him access to her core and her pleasure center. She moaned as he slide his finger in to the slick folds of her sheath. He finally lifted her and backed her up against the wall lifting her legs so she could wrap them around him. Reaching between them Lyssa found the opening in his pants and released his phallus. He was so hot; he gently placed her on his aching shaft. His heat and the pressure of his head penetrating her sheath made her moan. "Voltron she gasped."

He was never sorry that he had mated Lyssa she had been more to him than Elena had ever been, she had given him her love and his children. Her pleasure in their lovemaking filled his heart and made his manhood swell with desire. Finding the rhythm Voltron pumped her allowing the head of his shaft to pull the flesh down and then back up causing a delicious sensation. As the sensation increased their release was soon to follow. Lyssa cried out his name, pumping faster and faster Voltron felt his release very near, nuzzling Lyssa's neck he bit down as he released his seed deep into her womb, she cried out one more time as the bite sent tingling sensations down her spine into her clitoris. Voltron leaned into her slowly releasing her legs. When their breathing returned to normal Lyssa fixed the damaged their love making had done to her. Closing his pants he grabbed her hand and led her back to the chair.

"Well warrior I did not come to get ravaged but since you did then you must make an honest mate of me." She looked him right in the eyes.

Raising his eyebrow he took her hand and kissed it, "Well my lady I am afraid my mate would not appreciate me throwing her aside to keep you."

"Well my prince if you have a mate then I will have to leave you and find another to love me."

She turned to leave when Voltron growl and jump up to stop her retreat picking her up in his arms and twirling her around. Laughing she said, "Put me down warrior you make me dizzy." Laughing he sat her down on her feet kissing her sweetly on her forehead.

"I will be up in thirty minutes to dress for the ball. I need to finish this communication with the Milky Way galaxy. They had received a communication from them saying they had a couple in jail that fit the description of the want poster. After the celebration we need to fit the Erne for a voyage to the planet earth." Voltron told her.

Biting on her lip she said, "I will miss you so much."

"Why will you miss me you'll accompany me," He smiled, "I couldn't be away from you and our children that long. It will take one year to travel to the planet earth. My father and mother are coming as well. Would you like to invite your parents?" he asked sweetly as he picked up her hand and kissed it.

"Really?" she said excitedly. "Oh Voltron that would be wonderful I would love to get away from Zephron and see what is going on in the universe. I know," she said as she twirled around, "let's take

Nanny Nara and stop on the way at different planets I learned about in school." Clapping her hands, "Oh I can't wait Voltron." Rushing toward the door she blew him a kiss and left to get ready for the ball.

The Erne had left Zephron on star date 2027.37.017 they were half way across the universe in three months by the evening meal they would be going into the dark matter Galaxy Abell, it was a beautiful part of the universe with it colors and uncharted planets. After dinner Voltron and Lyssa sat in the commander's chair on the bridge and watched through the view screen as they passed the dark matter Galaxy. It truly was beautiful just sitting in the captain's chair relaxing in each other's arms and watching the universe go by.

It was early morning when Lyssa was awakened by Nara, Rylan had a high fever. Nara had placed a call to Belgorod telling him Rylan was sick please come to their quarters.

Scanning the baby Belgorod looked up concerned. "He has a ruptured appendix and needs surgery immediately." Placing his hand on Lyssa shoulder he smiled, "this is a really simple surgery Lyssa he will be fine."

She sent Nara to wake Voltron and let him know what was going on and to meet her in sick bay.

Pacing back and forth Lyssa couldn't sit still. Voltron went to her and placed his arms around her. Leaning back into him she let the tears fall. Going to the couch he sat down with her and held her. "You know this reminds me of the time I sat on this very couch waiting for Rylan to come into the world." She nodded. Taking a deep breath she laid her head back into his shoulder and closed her eyes.

"I should not have brought them on this mission. I am a bad mother they are just babies." She sobbed.

"Lyssa you are just tired. This would have happened back Zephron as well as here. You are the best mother I have ever known. Please don't cry." He had no sooner got those words out of his mouth than Belgorod came out of sick bay.

Jumping up Lyssa went to him with a look of concern on her face. "He is just fine Lyssa the medical unit was able to rid him of the infection from the rupture and to break up the appendix with sound waves. As soon as the unit seals the incision he can return with you to his crib."

"Thank you Belgorod." Rising on her tip toes she placed a kiss on his cheek. "Can I go in?"

"Let me make sure the unit is done. I will com you when it is."

"See I told you he would be fine."

"Yes you were right this time."

Sitting on the bridge Voltron waited for a communications from Tiernan. Lyssa had spent the whole night with Rylan and he found he had a hard time sleeping without her. Rylan was sleeping peacefully when he woke this morning and checked on him.

Roused from his thinking Arielle spoke, "Voltron I have Tiernan on the com screen."

Rising Voltron strode toward his ready room, "I'll take it in my ready room."

Sitting down he pushed the com vid screen and Tiernan appeared, "Voltron, how are you brother" he asked.

"I'm fine and you brother? I trust your journey to the Milky galaxy was informative?"

"Fine as well. I am just returning from earth and the couple they have in jail for galactic crimes is not Tess and Killian."

Shaking his head Voltron slammed his fist down on the table. "Damn I thought maybe we had them." He cursed.

"Voltron there is no need for you to continue to the Milky Way Galaxy. Galactic Intel tells me they are in the Blue Star Galaxy just at the edge of the Milky Way galaxy."

"What?" Voltron spoke, "we are just three weeks from that galaxy do you know which planet they are on?"

"They are on Micene. I will meet you there in three weeks, Tiernan out."

"Take care, brother."

Leaving the ready room Voltron told the bridge that he was going to the training room and to com him there if they needed him. Stopping on Deck 4 he was hopping Lyssa would want to go to the training deck with him and work out.

Entering their quarters he did not see her and went to the nursery to see if she was there. She and the babies were gone. Shrugging he turned to go to the bedroom where he changed into his training clothes. *She must be on the garden deck*, Lyssa had spoken to Voltron about using one of the lower decks as a garden spot, they could grow their own food, refresh their air supply and make a nice area for the warriors to go to and rest.

Entering the training bay Voltron noticed that all the warriors were huddled around something or someone. Moving closer to the group he couldn't believe his eyes, here were all his seasoned warriors cooing and awing over Brylan and Rylan. Arthur was holding Teagan with a big silly grin on his face. Walking up behind them he cleared his throat. Biden turned and saw Voltron standing behind him, rising quickly he leaned down and shook Colton's shoulder when he looked up he saw that Voltron stood behind Biden. Smiling Voltron moved them aside to see what was going on in the center of the circle.

"See Brylan, this is how daddy swings his sword when he is fighting our enemy." Lyssa was holding a set of small wooden swords that Arthur had carved for Brylan and Rylan. She was showing Brylan how Voltron held is sword. Brylan took the sword in his hand and lifted it up and over his head and swung out at the warriors in the circle. They all cheered him on as he continued to swing the little play sword. Rylan still recovering from his surgery sat quietly on his mother's lap watching as Brylan played with the sword. Looking up into Lyssa's eyes he said, "Momma where is sissyia's sword?"

"Arthur hasn't had time to make her one yet, right Arthur?" Lyssa said with a raised eyebrow looking directly at Arthur.

Arthur reddened under her gaze clearing his throat he spoke, "Yes Prince Rylan your mother is right I have not had time to make one for her." Turning he gave Teagan to Biden who was standing next to him. "I'll get right on that my prince." Turning he left to make Teagan a sword. He had not seen the snickering smile Voltron was trying to hide.

Rising from the floor Lyssa saw Voltron and smiled, "Rylan daddy is here you want to go with him to his training?"

Looking at his father he shook his head no, "No mommy I would rather stay with you can I?"

Seeing the disappointment in Voltron's eyes she looked down at her little son and smiled, "Yes that will be fine, Brylan do you want to go with daddy to his training?"

Jumping up and down Brylan started squealing, "Yes, yes I want to go with daddy." Smiling Voltron picked him up.

Looking at Teagan in Biden's arms Lyssa asked her, "Do you want to go with daddy to training?"

Smiling up at her mother Teagan spoke, "No mommy I want to go with Biden, please mommy can I go with Biden to his training?" Biden loved her adorable round rosy cheeks deep blue eyes and her soft blond hair streaked with blue black curls bobbing around her head as she asked enthusiastically.

Lyssa eyes got round as Teagan asked and Biden's cheek pinkened at the request. There was a tic in Voltron's cheek.

"Can I dada please?" she called him by her pet name instead of daddy. With her beautiful eyes pleading Voltron caved in.

"You can go with Biden because he will be training with me today. Aren't you Biden?" he asked with cold dark eyes.

"Yes, commander I am." To Teagan he smiled, "Teag," his pet name for the little princess, "You know your father is three times the warrior that I am. You should training with him."

Voltron looked at the young warrior and saw in his eyes that he loved the little princess, sighing he spoke. "Biden you can teach Teagan," saying her whole name to show is distain for him shortening it, "how to spar like her mother you do remember the moves right?" he asked.

Biden smiled, "Yes, commander I do." He bowed to Prince Voltron and Princess Lyssa and followed Voltron into the training gym. Lyssa got up with Rylan, hugging him close to her. "Are you tired Rylan?" shaking his head yes she kissed him on the forehead. "Alright then it's back to the nursery for you." with that she left the training bay as everyone let out a sigh of relief going back to their duties and training.

*   *   *   *

Lyssa and Voltron sat across the table from each other with Brylan and Teagan on his right and Rylan on his left. They were eating dinner together. Lyssa had told Voltron how important it was to her that her family have this time to share what they had done during their day. "How did training go with Brylan and Teagan?" she asked smiling lovingly at her husband.

Chewing the bite of meat he spoke, "We have a real little warrior in Brylan. He learned the moves from me as well as Biden."

"Did Teagan work with Biden on her moves?" she asked

"Yes for as little as they both are they were quick to learn the skills their mother had taught the other warriors."

"Oh, they were told I trained with the warriors?" she asked shocked.

"Yes, why is that so surprising?" he asked taking a drink of his grog.

Clearing her throat she spoke, "It's not surprising it just that after what went on before training I thought maybe you were displeased with me for taking them to the gym alone."

Placing his fork to his lips he had a quizzical look on his face when he asked, "Why would I be displeased with you?" he asked.

At that moment Rylan began crying. Getting up Lyssa went to him picking him up. "What's wrong? Rylan are you not feeling well?" she asked.

Sobbing he turned his head toward his father, "Why is daddy mad at you?"

Sucking in her breath she looked at Voltron. He rose quickly going to Lyssa and taking him in to his arms. "I am not mad at your mother little warrior. Why would you say that?"

"Because you sounded mad, mommy just wanted us to be like you. Why can't she take us to the gym and training room without you?" he asked turning his teary eyes to Lyssa then Voltron.

Rising with Rylan in his arms he felt chagrined that Rylan had picked up on his displeasure at Lyssa. Sitting down at his chair he looked lovingly at his children. "On our world men treasure our mates. I love your mother and I would never let anything hurt her or you. We protect our mates because we are afraid we might lose them to some other warrior stronger or better looking than us." He half way smiled until all the babies started giggling.

"Oh daddy," said Teagan, "You are more handsome than all your warriors and mommy loves you. Don't you mommy?" Teagan giggled.

Going to Voltron she kissed her handsome warrior on the lips smiling she said, "Yes Teagan I love your daddy very, very much. Now finish your dinner it is almost time for bed."

Voltron and Lyssa had just tucked the babies in and went to the sitting room to relax for a while.

"I had no idea Rylan was such an empathy. He's nothing like Brylan is he?"

"Nope, I was afraid when you found out you would be very upset. He may not be a warrior but I think he will make an excellent diplomat." She said handing him his drink.

Sitting beside him, "Teagan is going to be our other warrior. She is just like me when I was her age." Sipping her café mocha coffee she smiled at him.

"You are right of course, Brylan watches everything I do his little feet and hands followed every move I made today in the gym. When I saw that he was winded I wanted to stop but he shook his little head no."

"Yep he is just as stubborn as you." she giggled sitting her coffee down.

Pulling her on to his lap he kissed her passionately. "Stubborn am I?"

"Yes, look how long it took for you to finally fall in love with me." She said taking her hands and unbuttoning his shirt. Laying her head down she inhaled deeply. He smelled so good the musky spicy scent of a warrior.

Caressing her bodice he moaned as he took her soft breast into his hand.

Sliding off his lap she knelt between his legs unfastening his pants. As the pants opened his hard shaft sprung out in all its male glory. Looking into his eyes she saw they were heavy with desire.

Smiling she licked the head of his shaft tasting the sweet salty taste of his pre cum. Inhaling sharply he fisted the cushions as his hips bucked up to put more of his hot shaft into her mouth. Grabbing him with both her hands she pumped him until he groaned.

Grabbing her by the shoulders he lifted her and went to their room. Standing her on the floor he unbuttoned her bodice and let it fall behind her. Going to the waist of her skirt he undid it as well letting it fall to the floor.

Now it was her turn to pull his pants down but first she bent to unfasten his boots pulling the legs of his pants down off his feet. Rising she inhaled sharply as the heat emanating from his shaft nearly burned her hands. Looking up she saw that he was not going to play around tonight his need for her was too great.

Climbing up on the bed she laid back spreading her legs and invitation for him to come to her and make love to her. With one deep growl he placed his knee on the bed he lie down on top of her, kissing her cheeks, mouth and neck with his hungry mouth. Rising up he placed the head of his shaft at her entrance and thrust deep within the soft flesh. Moaning out as he did.

Wrapping her legs around his waist she met him thrust for thrust never taking her eyes off him. "I want you Voltron, my love, my warrior, and my life." Hearing her words of love made his entire body tremble with passion. Reaching down between their bodies he found her nub hard and ready. Rubbing his fingers over the sensitive spot made her cry out his name as she clung to him. He slowed his pace wanting to bring her again before he found his own release. Pulling almost out and thrusting back in all the while rubbing her nub he could feel her getting aroused. Burying his face in her neck he spoke breathlessly. "I want another baby my love." He had spoken so softly she almost hadn't heard him in her passion induced pleasure.

Lifting his head with her hands she kissed him deeply rushing the pace a little with her strong hips as she allowed him to ride her. Looking at her his kissed her deeply passionately as he sought his own release.

Lying beside her he spoke, "I love you so much Lyssa." Cradling her in his arms he covered them and fell asleep. His last thought was Zephron's lineage is well in the hands of his beautiful Lyssa.

Three weeks later they arrived at Micene. The investigation team transported to the surface of Micene just outside the city. The Intel told them Tess and Killian where staying in a long term caravansary called the Skyjack. Voltron had dressed as a dark warrior, with a flowing cape and mask to hide his identity. Lyssa dressed as a freebooter, wearing the tradition leather strap around her forehead with leather braided into her long hair. Her short tunic had a rope tied around the waist. She had her sword sheathed on her back hidden by the long cape that she tied around her neck. The outfit was completed by a pair of knee high leather boots with slots for her daggers. Tiernan wore the same outfit as Lyssa but in the style of the male freebooter. Arthur wore his ancient family clans tartans with his claymore strapped to his waist. The three would fit in with the miscreants of Micenia.

Micenia at one time had been a beautiful vacation planet but over the millennia had become home to freebooters, thefts, galactic miscreants. The smell of the city assuaged them long before they reached its walls. The smell of unwashed bodies, rotting food was incredible strong. Lyssa shudder at the smell and sights pulled her cape close about her. Sensing her fear Voltron moved a little closer to reassure her that he was there.

Once inside the city walls they split up and looked for the Skyjack. Unfortunately or fortunately depending on how you looked at it, Lyssa found the disreputable place first. She tried to com Voltron, but it seemed as if her communication link didn't work here. Pulling her mask down on her face she strode into the Skyjack and up to the bar.

The bartender eyed her before asking her what she wanted.

"A drink." She asked in a deep husky voice.

"What kind?" the bartender asked annoyed at her.

"A venutian gin." She said looking him straight in the eyes she dropped five silver dinaries on the bar as payment for the drink.

The bartender saw the great amount of money and smiled greedily as he poured her a drink, reaching for the money as he slide the glass to her. Smiling sweetly at her as sweetly as a filthy smelling unwashed alien could, he asked, "Anything else I can do for you?" sliding the wanted poster across the bar top she saw him pale. Picking up the poster he cleared his throat, putting his finger to his head he said, "I think they have gone from my place. Yes I am almost sure they left three days ago." He said sliding the poster back to her.

Picking it up she asked, "Are you sure, there is plenty more where that came from," she indicated the dinaries.

"How much more the greedy bar keep asked?"

"Let's just say enough if you answer correctly this time."

"Could I see the poster again?" he asked sheepishly.

Sighing she pulled it from her cape pocked and shoved it across the bar again. Waiting until he had picked it up she asked, "So are they here or not?"

This time his faced paled considerable. Following his eyes Lyssa looked to where the man was looking and saw her sister and Killian. Looking at her the bartender gave the poster back to her and left as quickly as his fat little legs could carry him.

Going to the table behind the three Lyssa sat down to listen to them.

"I told you that by sending that other couple posing as you and I to the planet called earth we would throw them off our tracks." Tess said snidely to Killian.

"Would you shut up?" Snapped Killian,

"Well Killian darling, if you had found better miscreants to help you Calum wouldn't have been killed and the two idiots that were left would have done their jobs." She glared back at him.

Voltron, Arthur and Tiernan had stopped on a back road trying to get their bearings. They hadn't heard from Lyssa in thirty minutes. In that time they had searched the area trying to find the Skyjack caravansary. Everyone they had asked about the Skyjack just looked at them and laughed at them.

Nara awoke to Rylan crying out. Going into the nursery she picked the little boy up, "Hush sweet Rylan what is the matter?" she spoke softly too him as she rocked him. "Mommy, mommy," he screamed out. Holding him at arm length Nara asked, "What is it Rylan?"

"Mommy's in danger." He cried. Lifting him up Nara went immediately to the com link and asked for the bridge to get Arielle.

They woke Arielle and sent him to his brother's quarters. "What is it Nara is Rylan sick again?"

"No, Prince Arielle Rylan says his mother is in danger."

Arielle looked at Nara like she had just grown two heads. "What are you saying?" he asked her not believe what he thought he heard.

"Princess Lyssa is in danger!" she said raising her voice.

"How? How does he know?"

"He has telepathic abilities. If you don't believe me ask him where his mother is right now."

Taking Rylan in his arms he sat on the couch with him. Looking at the little boy Arielle spoke softly to him, "Rylan where are mommy and daddy right now?"

"They are on Micene at a place called Skyjack." Getting agitated Rylan pushed on his uncle's chest. "Hurry Unca Ari mommy is in danger."

Arielle's eyes grew wide running to the bridge he opened communications with Voltron. "Voltron Lyssa is in danger."

"What? How do you know this?" Voltron asked anxiously.

"Rylan tell daddy where mommy is?"

"Daddy, mommy is in the Skyjack she is with a mean man named Killian and a woman named Tess . . . ," starting to cry Rylan said.

"It's ok Rylan daddy will take care of mommy."

The last person he asked started to laugh at them when Voltron grabbed him by the neck lifting him up off the ground. Slamming into the wall he bent and asked again where the Skyjack was. Shaking the man pointed to the road they were now on five blocks down the man said before passing out. Turning to Tiernan Voltron nodded with his head toward the road leading to the Skyjack. "To our left." He spoke softly.

Lyssa stared at Tess as she leveled the stun gun to Killian's chest. She watched as Killian sneered at Tess, "You can't do it can you Princess Tess." He taunted.

"Don't move or I will kill you." Tess said with deadly calm.

"Really Tess, are you sure you can kill me?" he asked with a smirk on his lips.

She took deadly aim and shot Killian in the chest.

Lyssa had heard enough, jumping up she flung her daggers at Tess. She screamed out in pain. "Why you little bitch." Pointing the gun at Lyssa she held her stance. Hatred streamed from her eyes.

Circling Tess Lyssa was trying to catch her off guard. "Oh it's so easy for you to kill me with a gun but you don't have the courage to kill me with a sword do you?" she taunted her sister. She had noted the look in Tess's eyes it was one of pure insanity. She knew she shouldn't keep taunting her but she had more of a chance with a sword than with a stun gun set on kill. Swallowing she looked at Tess again, "So are you going to kill me with the gun or fight me with a sword you coward."

Raising the gun higher Tess pointed the gun straight at Lyssa pulling the trigger. Lyssa heard Rylan scream get down mommy get down just as Tess pulled the trigger, missing Lyssa completely. At that moment Voltron roared through the door throwing his daggers straight into Tess's chest. She looked at him and then down at the daggers before she fell to the floor dead.

Rushing to Lyssa he hugged her tight. "What were you thinking, she could have killed you." he said again tightening his hold.

"She didn't though and you can thank our son, he yelled at me in my head to get down."

Pushing her back at arm's length he looked at her amazed. "What?"

"I heard Rylan yelling mommy get down. So I did."

"That's so amazing. Nara woke up Arielle because Rylan woke up and told her that you were in danger." Shaking his head he went on, "Can you believe that? He told us you were in the Skyjack and you were in trouble." He finished pulling her close again.

"I told you he was amazing." She smiled up at him.

Tiernan contacted the Erne. "Three to transport."

Arriving in the transportation bay Voltron lifted Lyssa and carried her to their quarters.

"Voltron, let me down I am not hurt I can walk." She squirmed trying to get out of his arms.

He just held her tighter. Looking at Tiernan he spoke. "I will be on the bridge in twenty minutes to file a report see you there.

Lyssa buried her face in Voltron's neck. *He's mad about something.* She shivered in his arms.

Arriving at their quarters he took Lyssa straight to their bedroom. Placing her on the bed he put his hands on his hips and glared at her. "You, little one, you are enough to make an Agathinian priest drink."

"I am sorry Voltron. I wasn't going to attack them until Tess killed Killian. Then I did so just so she wouldn't get away." She looked coyly at him.

Shaking his head he leaned down, "I love you but you scare the fires of Zephron out of me."

Kissing her he left. At the door he said huskily, "I'll be back soon. Wait to shower until I return."

She shivered again knowing that when he returned pleasure would be on the menu.

It had taken Voltron three hours to write the report and notify his father and Lyssa's father of the outcome of their search. Lyssa had fallen asleep waiting for him. Coming into their room quietly he saw that she slept, gently taking her clothes off her he then striped and got into bed beside her covering them both with the covers.

It felt like she had slept for hours. Stretching she felt Voltron's form next to her, she felt his arousal and rolled over to look into his eyes filled with desire. Taking her into his arms she kissed him deeply. She gently moved his hair off his forehead and looked deep into his eyes. "Do you remember when you said you were ready for another child?"

He shook his head yes. "Well," she said, "I am with your child again. Belgorod said this time there is only one baby."

Smiling he took her into his arms again kissing her passionately. Rubbing her arm he spoke, "Has Belgorod gotten any results of the testing he has been doing on our three children?"

"Yes, he says that the test results show the correlation between your bites and my fertility DNA caused me to conceive multiple babies and each of these babies then had special characteristic and growth rates cued to the mixture of DNA." Lying back onto the pillow she continued. "Belgorod thinks that because you only bit me once this pregnancy that this baby should be normal with no special characteristic." She sighed, "Kind of sad he should have special qualities like his siblings."

"Lyssa I have bitten you more than once, remember I bit you at least twice if not more during our love making." Sitting up quickly Lyssa looked at him confused, "You have?"

Nodding, "Yes at least twice. You don't remember because you were in the throes of passion my bite usually causes you to have extreme pleasure."

"I don't remember all of the bites then. Well this baby or babies then may have special qualities after all." She smiled lovingly at him. Tomorrow she would go to Belgorod and tell him that he had better scan her again. There just might be more than one baby again. Snuggling into him, she sighed heavily and fell asleep content.

Holding her close Voltron thought about the new baby or babies Lyssa was carrying and knew the lineage of Zephron was well on its way. He smiled as he held her close and kissed her hair before falling asleep himself.